Close to Destiny

a novel

ADRIA J. CIMINO

Published by Velvet Morning Press

ISBN-13: 978-0692346945
ISBN-10: 0692346945

Cover design by Vicki Lesage and Ellen Meyer
Author photo by Didier Quémener

To Didier, my inspiration

PART I

July 1

It was my third time. Don't they always say things happen in threes? Knife slitting through fragile skin, still damp.

Water pounding like giant teardrops. Sitting at the edge of the bathtub, knees shaking, watching scarlet water flow.

Darkness. Silence.

What seemed like a second turned into eternity. Blinding light. Voices. Madness. Silence.

That's all I could write, all I could remember. I didn't want to think about it. I didn't want to analyze the situation or understand why.

Six months later

"It looks ravishing on you! How could you possibly hesitate?"

I whirled around, nearly knocking over a hat rack sandwiched between shelves overflowing with gloves and sweaters. A man of about 40 was studying me out of the corner of his eye as his fingers examined a stack of cashmere scarves. We were the only customers in the shop, which was beginning to feel like a particularly small broom closet.

"You thought you were alone?" he continued, pushing up the sleeves of his long black overcoat. "I know it's not that common—most stores are closed after all—but I love shopping on the first day of the year. Always have. It's the best way to avoid the crowds."

He placed a scarf against the arm of his tweed jacket, grimaced, set it back on the shelf, and turned to face me.

"So what's the verdict?"

My hands toyed with the black velvet hat. It had beckoned to me as I plodded along the sidewalk a few minutes earlier, dragging my suitcase and wishing it wasn't so damn cold in London. Now, I tried it on once again. I felt almost lightheaded as I took one nervous glimpse of myself in the mirror.

"There's no reason to wait another minute!" the man said, golden cat-like eyes flashing. "You can't say it isn't beautiful, can you?"

"No, no, it's not that," I said dully. "I just feel kind of odd, that's all."

The man glanced toward the door.

"Is that your suitcase?"

I nodded.

"You've traveled here from the States, haven't you?"

I nodded again.

"How could you expect to feel anything other than odd after such a trip?"

I grinned, both perplexed and amused by his comments, then turned back to the mirror. The hat's rim squashed red ringlets that later escaped like springs around my ears. My fingers rubbed against the plush velvet.

"I'll take it," I said decisively.

"It's already taken care of," a chipper voice said behind me. I turned to the saleswoman, who offered me a silver bag with a bright purple handle. "You can carry it home in the bag or wear it if you'd prefer…"

Then, obviously noticing my confusion, she nodded toward the door. My eyes followed. The man was strolling down the sidewalk. He turned back to us all of a sudden, lifted his umbrella as if toasting with a glass of champagne, then disappeared around the corner.

Once in my hotel room, I stuffed the hat and its mounds of tissue paper into the back of the closet and wondered if I would wear it, or if it would become yet another one of the useless items I had been collecting ever since I needed a distraction from reality.

January 2

I could no longer ignore it. An incessant tapping at the door that even the thickest feather pillow couldn't camouflage. My toes sank into the carpet as I wandered through the unfamiliar darkness. The glimmer of the room-service button on the phone guided me. I unlocked the door and swung it open in a fury.

Drawing in a sharp breath, I took a step back. Was I dreaming? Had I finally gone crazy? I blinked twice, but that didn't change the landscape.

A naked woman was still standing there right in front of me. Her large hazel eyes were glazed and curious, and she didn't seem at all bothered by the situation. Some might have found this scenario intriguing—and I knew of a few who would consider it a perfect opportunity for a one-night adventure. But for me, it was more of an annoyance than anything else. Especially since I had come to this place to get my life back together. I didn't have time to be woken up by naked women at 3 a.m., and I told her as much. Her response sent a shiver up my spine.

"You're not ready? I don't agree. Think things over, Katherine."

"How do you know my name?"

My shaky words were too late. She had already disappeared around the corner. That's what brought me to my journal at such a late hour. Who could sleep after such an encounter?

It was difficult enough for me to be here in this dim hotel that loomed high with its post-modern design on a slim, quiet cobblestone street. I could have searched through the halls that snake in maze-like form through the circular structure. But they would have been empty, as they were even in the middle of the day. This place gave me the impression that I was completely alone.

I wouldn't have been able to stay here a month ago. No, I was too fragile then. Even now, I hated the silence and isolation. But it wasn't as if I had much of a choice. The Grand East Hotel wanted to exhibit my work in two different phases over the next few months. Those strange charcoal drawings I had done when my only human contact was Dr. Bell. The expression of my internal suffering on paper would apparently please the wealthy business travelers, who might pay well into the hundreds to bring a bit of the sadness home.

I didn't swallow the bullshit about this being part of the healing process. Refusing to dwell on the past was the best strategy. I was convinced of it, even if Dr. Bell said I should use the experience to look inward. I shuddered at the thought. This was about moving forward. A vacation from my twice-weekly visits with him would do me good.

Paul didn't want me to come here. He turned his back on me when I was at my lowest, and the worst part was he didn't realize it. He thought I had control. *"We don't have to live this way!"* Those words repeated themselves painfully in my mind. He didn't have time to listen or understand. Then he would say "I love you," and I would tell him the same, although I wasn't sure about anything any more. A vacation from Paul would do me good as well.

Tomorrow—well, actually in a few hours—I would meet with Gwen Garnier, the art consultant organizing this whole project. Dr. Bell introduced me to her back in New York only a few weeks ago, but I felt as if I had known her a lot longer. I liked her frank way of speaking. She was the first one to openly criticize Dr. Bell in front of me. She said his technique was too scholarly: He was dealing with human beings, but sometimes he treated them more like text books with arms and legs. So I decided to put my faith in Gwen when she asked me to participate in the art exhibit. I had to think of this as an opportunity.

A fluttering burst of laugher made me drop my journal to the ground. My heart pounded as I ran to the door. Could it be that woman yet again? I tentatively slipped into the hallway. Empty. Not a sign of life. The grayish light lent an eerie glow to the stark white walls. I returned to my room. Who was that visitor after all? How did she know my name, and what was she trying to tell me?

January 3

Gwen met me for breakfast at one of the hotel's restaurants at 9 a.m. sharp. She kept the earpiece of her cell phone in one ear to catch all calls immediately. At the same time, she managed to flirt with the waiter through her lilting French accent, butter a slice of toast and study me as if my freckled face was a work of art. I sank back into my chair and studied the globs of oatmeal swirled with honey. Food still had a way of making me nervous. I pushed the bowl aside, and looked back at Gwen's bright eyes, framed by short, wavy blond hair.

"I would like you to really take part in this exhibit, Kat," she said. "It's always most interesting when the artist is there to talk about his or her work."

"I hate public speaking."

She shook her head and broke out her kindest smile.

"Nothing intimidating, of course… I'm talking about one-on-one conversations. You'll spend a couple of hours at the exhibit each day so that visitors can come over and chat with you."

"I can't tell them what the drawings mean."

"That's all right," she said. "They won't expect you to pour out your soul. Visitors understand the context of this kind of exhibit."

I felt my face go scarlet. Gwen put her hand on my arm.

"There is no reason to feel embarrassed…"

"By the fact that everyone will be thinking I'm some kind of nut?"

Again she shook her head.

"Kat, no one is one hundred percent stable all of the time. The ability to produce something artistic in a moment of angst is impressive. That's why I'm in the business of showing this kind of art, and that's why people buy it."

I twirled a long strand of rebellious hair around my finger and looked at Gwen skeptically, yet I was not tempted to end the whole deal. I still couldn't help being intrigued by the idea of showing these rather ugly charcoal drawings. Maybe someone else would appreciate them more than I did. I wanted to satisfy my curiosity.

"How do you like the hotel?" Gwen asked.

"Other than the middle-of-the-night visitors, I guess it's OK."

"What do you mean?"

I hesitated. Gwen took a quick phone call, laughed, explained away a problem with alacrity, and returned her attention to me. No, I couldn't tell her about my experience. She would think it was ridiculous and nothing more than a silly dream. I would have to handle the situation on my own.

∽◦∾

I tapped my fingers in agitation on the marble desk as I waited for the whiny-sounding attendant to finish her phone conversation. Yes, the hotel is a block away from the tube, and yes, there still is a room for two available this weekend. Mmhm, mmhm. She nodded and noted information in the reservation book with looping swoops of her thin hand. Finally, she hung up and turned her rather tired-looking, round face to me.

I told her I was staying in room 405 and that I had had a bit of a noise problem the previous night.

"Ah, the plumbing. Yes, the showers and toilets are a bit loud because we have a special system that is environmentally friendly…"

I cut her off.

"No, it's not that," I insisted. "Someone was knocking on my door for about ten minutes in the middle of the night, and when I dragged myself out of bed to see who exactly was making such a commotion, I found myself face-to-face with a naked woman!"

The girl looked taken aback.

"I don't know of any such thing. Our hotel is very respectable."

"Well whatever type of hotel you have, I'm telling you there was a naked woman walking the halls last night. Whether she's a call girl or…"

"We don't ever have…"

"You obviously know very little about what the hotel does and doesn't have," I said. A sarcastic laugh escaped from within. I felt as if my cheeks were turning the same color as the unruly hair that I flipped over one shoulder. I became assertive all of a sudden. I knew exactly what I had seen.

"Look, it's clear you're not going to admit anything, but don't say it isn't true. You're better off saying nothing." I smirked and shook my head. The girl seemed dazed, unprepared for a confrontation that didn't resemble any of the trial ones tested on her before she took the job.

"I think you should be aware that there's a tall, thin woman, in her late 20s it seems, with long brown hair who just so happened to be banging on my door last night. If you see a guest who fits that description, you might want to find out what she's doing here."

"I'll be on the lookout," the girl said in a stilted voice. "Our job is to assure our guests' well-being."

But it was obvious she only wanted to get rid of me and return to the fan magazine I saw hastily stuffed under a tourism brochure. No use wasting any more time there. It was a losing battle. Plus, for the first time in a long while, I had work to do. Gwen would be meeting me a half hour later to start setting up the exhibit.

January 8, night

My heart was beating double time as I opened the door. I knew she was there. Maybe I should have called the security desk and put an end to this ridiculous situation. But I couldn't. Something about it fascinated me too much to stop it.

She was wearing a long, sky-blue beaded dress and her hair was twisted into a chignon with a feather clip. She didn't explain the reason for such a transformation from her initial appearance. In fact, she didn't say a thing about our first encounter.

"What's this really all about?" I asked, stepping into the hallway. I was standing there in my billowy nightgown like Wendy in *Peter Pan*. I had my journal in the front pocket, and I gripped it with one hand, as if it would give me strength.

"I want you to meet some friends of mine," she said. "We're having quite a lovely party. Come along…"

She took me by the hand, led me swiftly right, left, up a flight, then down another, around a few corners, into an empty room, and finally to what looked like a ladder scaling one wall. I followed. My bare feet awkwardly gripped each step. Jazzy music wafted into my ears from above. She arrived at the top and pulled me with her through a large square of darkness pierced only by flashing lights.

We were sitting on our knees on hardwood floors. At the feet of a bartender. His well-polished shoes going through almost a tap dance routine from right to left. I realized we were behind a bar. Champagne was flowing. She stood up and pulled me along with her. Beyond the zinc counter, the dance floor was packed. Stars glowed through bay windows lining the far wall. The bartender didn't seem to notice us as he handed out glass after glass.

The band played *Sing! Sing! Sing!* I hadn't heard that tune since those long afternoons at my grandma's house so many years ago. Dresses of taffeta, silk and sequins swayed as men rolled up their sleeves and twirled their partners around the floor. Disco balls and flashes of light turned the trombone pink, green and silver in sequence before puffs of smoke swallowed up my view of the band.

Then, out of the haze, he emerged. He couldn't have been much older than me, but he had a presence that seemed ageless. It wasn't the stylish velvet tuxedo jacket or the expensive watch that drew everyone's eyes to him. After all, the people staying at this place wore their share of luxury goods. No, it was something indescribable. He brushed back his silky, dark hair with one hand and touched the arm of his partner, a doe-eyed blond, with the other.

"Well if it isn't Destiny!" he said in a smooth, melodious voice. I stood there dumbly as he arrived in front of us and kissed my guide on both cheeks. His partner stepped back. I saw hostility in the large green eyes.

"Sam, be sociable," he said, and then turned his million-dollar smile to me.

I didn't know what to say. I didn't even know what I was doing there. And to make matters worse, I remembered that I was wearing a nightgown at a most-elegant party. But none of this seemed to matter to him.

"I'm Gabriel, and this is my darling Sam," he said. Sam grinned at me. A tender, likeable face. "Are you one of my sister's new friends?" Gabriel continued. "She's always meeting people…"

Destiny took control of the situation. She placed a delicate hand on my shoulder.

"Yes, you can say we're becoming friends," she said. "We met downstairs. I thought she would enjoy seeing the other side of this place. Your parties are always unforgettable."

"That's my sister for you," Gabriel said. "I can do no wrong."

I forced a pleasant look onto my face. I felt awkward, out of place. Only glancing at Sam made me feel a bit better. He seemed the most like me among all of these strangers. Sam remained beside Gabriel, but refused to look at Destiny. His eyes were distant.

"But that's not all," Destiny was saying.

"Oh really?" Gabriel replied, feigning surprise.

"She has to meet Will. He's here, isn't he?"

Gabriel nodded.

"I saw him earlier, at the far end of the room."

Destiny took my hand. But suddenly, the smoke from the dance floor was overwhelming me. I couldn't move forward. I couldn't move backward. I was trapped. I wanted to scream. I thought I was fainting. Memories of the last failed attempt to end it all flooded my head. Did someone drug me? I didn't drink anything... And then the world went dark.

I scribbled down everything in great haste after groggily waking up at 6 a.m. in my hotel bed. I had to remember every detail. Was I going crazy? Everything had to be a dream. But why was I having these insane dreams? Maybe that visit from a naked woman the other night—Destiny—was a dream. No wonder the hotel staff looked at me like I was a complete nutcase. The receptionist must have told everyone about my bizarre complaint. I jumped out of bed and ran to the mirror. The bathroom tile cooled my feet. I was overheated. My normally pink complexion was raspberry, and my hair was standing on end. I inhaled and exhaled slowly—one, two, three times. I was going to take a shower, go downstairs and tend to my exhibit. I had to forget about Destiny. She was a figment of my imagination. Nothing more.

January 11

Gwen noticed that I hadn't been eating. She took me by the arm and propelled me to the hotel restaurant, where she ordered club sandwiches and fries. She meant well, but that was hardly the type of meal that appealed to me. I was having a rough time looking at the overloaded plates placed before us. I felt nauseated. That wasn't a good sign. I had to resist, but the familiar voice inside my head sprung to life once again.

"You have to fight this, Kat," Gwen was telling me. "I don't understand... You were doing so well. But all of sudden, you've turned inward."

I took a deep breath and reached for a French fry. I chewed it slowly, painfully. The fry made it down. Then another. I closed my eyes and felt the thick, grainy texture. I didn't want to be there. I didn't want to be anywhere. I thought of the phone messages Paul had left for me. At least three of them. I couldn't go back there either. I wasn't ready to face him again, yet the thought of losing him terrified me.

"I'm fine," I said unconvincingly. Gwen didn't know about my tumultuous relationship with Paul. And I didn't feel like explaining.

"Kat, what exactly is going on?" Gwen's eyes were flashing. "Our exhibit is about to open and you're heading into some kind of crisis? The purpose of this isn't to pressure you... Please tell me if that's the problem!"

"I've been having disturbing dreams," I blurted out. That

wasn't the whole truth, because I still wasn't 100 percent convinced that my encounters with Destiny weren't real.

"It's more than that," she said. "I can tell."

She leaned forward and studied me with intense eyes. I wished I could disappear. I knew Gwen wouldn't let me off the hook until I spilled at least one secret.

"A strange woman has come to my door twice in the middle of the night," I whispered. "I don't know why. I don't understand what she wants from me... or if she wants anything at all. I followed her once, to this amazing party... and then, somehow, I ended up back in my bed. Don't ask me how. So what do you think of this? Reality or fantasy?"

Gwen raised her eyebrows and settled back in her chair.

"Only you can answer that question, Kat."

"You think I've got a screw loose, don't you?"

"No." Gwen took a sip of her diet Coke and gazed into the distance. She was analyzing the situation, but remained completely poker faced. I wanted her to say something, to offer me some advice or guidance.

"What would you do?" I asked desperately.

"I would see if she returns."

"You think she is real, then? You actually believe this craziness?"

"Kat, there are some things in life that we have to deal with on our own. You're ready to do so... You are recovering. Only these past couple of days have weakened your spirit. You can't let that happen!"

I gazed down at my plate and weakly attempted to chew on a corner of bread and overcooked bacon. Many months had passed since my last breakdown, but it was a continuous battle. For the moment, though, I maintained control. I ate a quarter of the sandwich and four fries. It took me forever to stuff all of this unwelcome food down my throat. But I succeeded. I refused to vomit. I felt disgusting, but I was making progress. This would be my twelfth week of what most would consider "normal" behavior.

I wondered if Gwen knew more about Destiny than she was willing to admit. I pushed her on the subject, but she wouldn't budge. Her eyes were unreadable. I could already tell that Gwen was used to having the upper hand in relationships. I would be silly if I thought I could decipher what was going on in her mind.

She was smiling at me and telling me to meet her in the gallery that evening at 6 p.m. to prepare for the opening. I felt my heartbeat quicken. Until that moment, my nightly experiences nearly pushed the excitement of the art exhibit out of my mind. Everything was happening so quickly. Too quickly. I was nervous, yet eager to launch this show. Maybe it was what I needed to pull me away from thoughts of Destiny.

January 12, in the wee hours

It was as if I were in the haze that comes over me when I've had one too many. The feeling of moving in slow motion. God-only-knew-how-many people were fluttering around my drawings as well as the works of others. Silky, black cocktail dresses and dark suits become one mass of excitement as they spun around me. We had been there for hours, and the crowd was nonstop. They told me they loved my work. Whether this was true or not, it did make me feel good. I actually enjoyed the brief conversations and was happy to get my mind off recent preoccupations.

After speaking with so many of these visitors, I gratefully retreated to anonymity. I saw Gwen in the distance, in distracted conversation with several people at once. She was beckoning to me, but a hand on my arm stopped everything. All activity seemed to come to a standstill. Destiny was at my side. She was wearing another formal gown; this time a long, satin amethyst number that billowed out like an elegant cape. I swallowed hard and looked around. Eyes were on us, but Destiny didn't seem to notice.

She took my arm.

"Come with me, Katherine, I have someone you must meet."

I wanted to resist, to see what she would do, but I was physically unable to do it. My feet glided forward, and in minutes, we were at the top of the ladder that we had climbed together the other night. Again, we were on our knees behind the bar.

"Who are these people, and what are we doing here?" I asked. Finally, my voice had returned. "What do you want with me anyway?"

Destiny gazed at me calmly. There was a comforting, almost magical aura about her. "I want you to meet Will."

The name rang a bell. I remembered hearing it before I faded out the last time.

"Who's Will, and why do you want me to meet him?"

"You'll find out," she said, patting me on the hand.

Then we stood up and moved forward. The scene was much the same as that of the other evening. Gabriel and Sam were involved in an intense conversation as gyrating bodies decked in baubles and beads moved to the beat of the drums. I followed Destiny through the haze of smoke until we reached one of the bay windows. Below, London's winding cobblestone streets were dark and sleepy.

I looked up and my heart skipped a beat. Destiny had disappeared. I didn't want to be left here alone. A soft male voice interrupted my internal panic.

"I'm Will," he said as he took my hand. "Destiny wanted to introduce us, but I see she's rushed off to yet another emergency."

He had dark brown hair, blue eyes and a kind smile. Had I seen him somewhere before? I felt comfortable with him. I racked my brain, but couldn't come up with a thing. We were closer together all of a sudden, but I don't remember either of us stepping forward.

"What do you mean by emergency?" I asked, figuring I could find out more about our mysterious friend.

"Oh, Destiny always seems to be helping someone out of trouble," Will said vaguely. "People trust her."

"Why did she want us to meet?"

"You should ask her that."

"You know. But you won't tell me?"

"I promised I would leave the explanations to her."

I should have been annoyed, but I wasn't. How could I possibly be? Those eyes captivated me so…

"Do you know how to get out of this place?" I finally said. "This is the second time she's taken me here, but I'm sure I couldn't find an exit on my own."

Will grinned.

"I know the way, and I'll be at your side," he said.

I was grateful that the dimming lights masked the several shades of red that must have colored my face, but I turned away all the same.

"I didn't mean to embarrass you."

"That's OK," I said, my voice a whisper. "Everything about this situation is odd. How do you know Destiny, anyway? Can you at least tell me that? Who is she really?" I ran a hand through my hair and closed my eyes. "I mean, how does she know who I am and why has she been coming to my room? Who are these people and why are we here with them? I don't understand any of it."

"I've known Destiny for a few years," Will said. "I used to travel through London frequently. We met one day when I was doing some research here at one of the libraries. Now, I spend most of my time in New York, but of course, whenever I'm in London, I pay her a visit."

"But who is she?"

"She's a young woman with a lot of spirit."

His eyes were dancing, and I couldn't help being drawn closer to him.

"And who are you?" I asked. "We haven't met before, but I feel as if we have. Maybe back in New York? No, I would have remembered. Or, maybe I'm going completely bonkers."

Will pulled me close to him, and I felt his lips touch mine. My heart was racing. A fleeting thought of Paul disappeared. The room was spinning. I didn't want this moment to end— ever. Maybe it would have gone on forever if it hadn't been for the sound of angry voices. It was as if the whole place fell silent so that Sam's voice could ring out loud and clear.

"It's your fault, Destiny! Don't you see?"

"Honey, stop," Gabriel was saying, running a hand along the back of Sam's shirt. "We're together right here and now. That is what's important."

But Sam was ignoring him.

"If you can't control everything, then why do you pretend to? Is it selective with you? I'm tired of this lifestyle, Destiny!" The pain in his voice made my heart ache.

"I know, Sam," she murmured. "I am too, but we don't have much of a choice."

I was riveted to the scene, but in a matter of seconds, Will grabbed my hand, and we were flying across the floor and down the trap. I didn't want to leave, yet I was afraid to stay. I followed Will's hurried steps.

And then our fingers slid apart. I don't know how, but I lost him. In this fucking maze of a hotel, I lost him.

Early morning

I couldn't stop thinking of Will. I could still feel his soft brown hair brushing through my fingers, his mouth against mine, the intensity of his gaze. All of these images and sensations were strangely familiar. I didn't understand it. The only thing I knew was I had to see him again. But how? In the back of my mind, I felt a slight twinge of guilt. Paul was back in New York waiting for me, and I still hadn't returned his messages. I promised myself I would call him that evening. In any case, I wasn't necessarily planning on getting involved with Will. I simply wanted to comprehend everything that had been happening.

The doorbell rang. Room service. Tea, toast, yogurt and strawberries.

"I didn't order this," I said.

"Oh, I know," the girl replied, her blond ponytail bobbing as she nodded. "It's from a friend."

"Who?"

She looked down at a note in her hand. "Hmm... It says here: From someone who wants you to stay well. That's it."

I knitted my brow. Probably Gwen, afraid I was going to relapse.

After the girl left, I chewed on a piece of dry toast and sipped a cup of Ceylon. Every meal was an effort for me. One strawberry. Two teaspoons of yogurt. I used to count the calories. I knew exactly how many were in everything from a potato chip to a pop tart. This time, I resisted the temptation. Instead, I kept thinking of Will. I had the right to want to know more about him. Paul screwed around plenty and at the worst of times. Just the thought sickened me. My quest was an innocent one. I decided to make my way back to the site of last night's party. I pulled on a pair of jeans and a sweater, and hurried out the door before I had time to change my mind.

As usual, the halls were empty and dim. Slowly, I retraced the steps we had taken in the opposite direction only hours earlier. It was as if the hallways were part of a maze, turning left, right. Then there was a door to enter another wing. Finally, I neared my destination. I saw the ladder. In my sneakers, I scampered up. At the top, a board blocked the entrance. I grasped it, but the panel wouldn't budge. My heart was racing. I had to see what was behind it. I pushed the board with all of my strength, and sailed into the room in one sudden burst. There was sawdust everywhere. I coughed and rubbed my eyes. Workbenches, tubs of paint, stepladders and every tool one could imagine littered the room. The place was under renovation! I felt as if my heart was going to jump out of my chest. I didn't get it. I was numb. I crossed the floor and stood at the bay window where Will had kissed me. Tears filled my eyes. Was all of this—every part of it—a dream? A feeling of loss overwhelmed me.

I heard footsteps coming from a long hallway that I had never noticed. I froze as two figures emerged. They were workmen, carrying more tubs of paint and laughing raucously.

"You lost, young lady?" one of them asked as he adjusted his cap with a chubby hand.

"More and more with every minute," I said, almost to myself. "What is this place anyway? Does anyone use it?"

The men laughed as they set down their supplies.

"You kiddin'? As it is, you better make yourself scarce… It's dangerous to be hanging around a work site, you know."

"But I've… heard people up here at night. That's why I wanted to check it out."

"The only things running 'round here at night are mice," the younger and slimmer painter said. "After all, the only way you can get up here is by a ladder and a couple of wooden trap

doors—you must know that. And you have to be in the hotel
first. Now, I don't know why any hotel guest would want to
spend an evening up here!"

I had to get out. I ran across the room, squeezed through
the crawl space and stumbled down the ladder. The painters
must have been shaking their heads in confusion, but I
wouldn't turn back. It was over. I had proof that everything
had been part of my stupid imagination.

As I scribbled the whole experience into my journal,
teardrops tumbled onto the pages, turning black ink into liquid
smudges.

ৡৣৡ

I wanted to spend hours in bed crying and hiding my face
from the light of day. But I couldn't. I had to get out of The
Grand East Hotel. At least for a few hours. I was going stir
crazy in the quiet dimness! I wanted to go back to New York
and forget about everyone and everything I had come across
here in London. But I couldn't do that either. I bundled
myself up in the black wool coat that fell like an A-line dress
to my knees. I was about to close the door to the wardrobe
when the corner of a silver bag, tossed hastily in the corner,
caught my eye.

The hat. It wouldn't be a useless acquisition after all. I
tucked my hair under the brim and glanced into the mirror.

"It looks ravishing on you!" The words echoed in my
head. But it wasn't the voice of the man who'd bought me the
hat. It was another voice. Familiar, but I couldn't identify it.
Over and over, the words expanded in my mind, reaching a
deafening crescendo. I swallowed hard and studied my
reflection. The lightheadedness I had felt in the shop violently
overcame me. I yanked off the hat and collapsed onto the bed.

I was frozen solid even though I was covered up as if for
a winter in Antarctica. Slowly, I glanced at the hat and shook
my head. I knew I was being ridiculous. It was a perfectly
beautiful hat, so why wouldn't I hear my own inner voice
commenting on it? I was the one driving myself insane.

I sat up, took the hat gently in my hands and tucked it into the silver bag. Once my mental state improved, I would wear it. For the moment, it seemed as if I had created some sort of bizarre fixation… at least that's what Dr. Bell likely would have said.

Taking a deep breath, I left the room, walked briskly through the hallways and out the revolving front door. I pushed the hat episode to the back of my mind. The icy air filled my lungs. I'd become too accustomed to the constant heat of the hotel. There wasn't much on this street other than a few pubs, but around the corner there was a complex of shops. I wandered in and out of a few to pass time. Only the bookstore was of any interest to me. I smacked 15 pounds onto the counter and bought a book about interpreting dreams. I felt this might somehow give me a bit of control in a situation that had left me powerless and confused.

Book in hand, I crossed the street to a whimsical looking tearoom with purple doors and shutters. It was crowded, but I found a tiny glass table and a plush lavender chair at the back of the room.

"Welcome to Violet's Tea Dream, may I take your order?" a breathless lilting voice said. "Our specialty is violet tea and violet scones."

"That'll be fine," I said, still digesting the unusual décor. I was the lone tea drinker of the bunch. Mothers and daughters, friends and couples sat at each table. A flowery scent—most likely the violets—filled the air. It calmed me. I took a deep breath and turned to chapter one. At the same time, the waitress set a silver teapot, a silver-rimmed china cup and a fragrant, lavender-tinged scone on the lace placemat before me. My eyes returned to the printed page, but before I could finish reading the first sentence, a strange feeling overwhelmed me. I looked up.

"You know those kinds of books are useless, don't you?" Destiny slid into the chair next to mine. "Fifteen pounds out the window," she continued with a grin. "But if it amuses you…" She sighed and shook her head.

My hands were trembling. The book fell to the floor. I was simultaneously hot as an oven and ice-cold. I didn't know if seconds or minutes had passed, but it felt like forever. The waitress reappeared and told Destiny she would bring "the usual."

"You come here often?" I mumbled. I was shocked that my voice was actually able to make it out of my throat.

"This is my tearoom," she said. Destiny picked up my book, dusted it off and set it on the table. "I meant what I said about these kinds of books... a total waste of money!" Shamefully, I stuffed my recent purchase into my backpack.

Destiny poured a cup of tea and handed it to me. I took a sip, not wanting to offend her.

"Delicious," I said, but my mind was far from the taste of violet tea.

I took a deep breath. I couldn't be dreaming. Destiny was right here with me in broad daylight. The waitress saw her after all. And she looked so normal. An ordinary young woman sitting down for an afternoon snack. Out of the corner of my eye, I looked her up and down. Today, she was wearing a long, blue dress—rather plain compared with her usual attire.

"So you are real," I said.

"Of course I am," she said with a laugh.

"This is really uncomfortable, but I have... some questions... I'm confused. I mean, how do you know me? Who are those friends of yours and how can they have a party in a room that's being renovated? And Will? Who is he, and why did you want me to meet him?" I hoped I didn't sound hysterical, but I could hardly restrain my feelings.

The waitress returned with Destiny's tea and scone, and disappeared in a matter of seconds. Destiny looked at me with kind, understanding eyes.

"Oh, initiation is always difficult," she said. "But it's the only road."

"Initiation into what?"

Destiny took a delicate bite of her scone and a sip of tea, then pondered for a moment.

"I was a bit presumptuous when we first met, so I've decided to take a step back. You're not ready to hear everything, or understand everything yet, Kat, but the one thing I can tell you is that Will is not a figment of your imagination, and you'll be meeting him again—that is, if you want to."

"I do want to see him." Elation filled my heart, but I told myself to hold back this silly feeling of joy. I couldn't plunge into anything.

"Yes, but there's some hesitation too. You don't want to rush."

"How did you know that?" I asked.

"It's written all over your face."

"Destiny…" I said her name awkwardly, like a child getting used to the sound of a new word. "Why did you choose me for whatever it is you're doing?"

She laughed and touched my hand lightly.

"I didn't choose you, Katherine. Things have a way of unfolding and guiding us in certain directions. I can't turn my back on my responsibilities."

I felt more in the dark than before our conversation. Most of my questions had gone unanswered.

"Don't be discouraged, Katherine. I told you that you had to meet Will, and that worked out splendidly. The rest will too."

She took a final sip of tea, told me my order was on the house, smiled brilliantly and headed out the door. I stared at my uneaten scone and the crumbs Destiny had left behind. Feelings of relief, confusion and frustration entwined. What right did Destiny have to play with my life? How had she managed to take such control in a period of days? I held my head in my hands, hoping the headache that was starting to creep up would go away.

∽∾

The damn receptionists at the hotel made my blood boil. I asked them if they had a guest named Will or William—an American—and they refused to give me any information whatsoever. Privacy reasons.

I tried hanging out in the lobby. An hour passed. Nothing. Now, it was an hour before my dinner meeting with Gwen. I was in the gallery, organizing business cards from people who wanted more information about the artwork in our show. Gwen had prepared price sheets and other materials, so I had the feeling I would be doing a lot of mailings. Spending an hour here would be good for me. It would keep my mind on the art project and that alone.

"Kat!" Gwen's voice startled me, and I nearly jumped out of the leather chair. I was sitting in a shadowy alcove that we used as our office. Here, we were cut off from the world. Gwen sat on the stool opposite me and gripped the edge of the eighteenth century mahogany desk that separated us. "What happened last night?"

Her voice was serious and her eyes wide.

"What are you talking about?" I asked, shaking my head. "Didn't everything go OK?"

"This isn't about the show, Kat. It's about Destiny."

"What?" I swallowed hard.

"How do you know her and where did she take you?"

"Wait a minute... I don't get it." I was talking to myself, yet out loud.

"You can't possibly know her very well... No one does. She doesn't let anyone get very close."

"You know Destiny? You recognized her last night?"

I leaned forward and didn't take my eyes off Gwen. I was afraid I would miss a necessary clue if I turned my attention away for a second. Apparently, she hadn't realized that Destiny was the rather eccentric visitor I spoke of yesterday. Or if she did make the link, she was keeping the discovery to herself.

"Her family is very wealthy," Gwen said. "But they stay out of the public eye. No one knows much about them or their investments, and it's best that way."

Suddenly, I remembered my conversation with the hotel receptionist. Of course, she knew I was referring to Destiny walking the halls naked in the middle of the night. That's why she was uncomfortable! She wouldn't dare cross one of the hotel's rich guests.

"Anyway, the one thing I do know about her is that she's an art lover, and fellow art lovers here in London tend to use her as a guide. If Destiny buys an artist's work, everyone follows. Six months later, the artist is a star, and Destiny has moved on to other things. So the idea of her setting foot in the gallery…"

Gwen gazed dreamily up at the gray ceiling as if looking at a perfect blue sky. Then she asked me if Destiny had said anything about her or commented on our show. But I didn't want to share my stories of Destiny with her. I had to handle the situation on my own.

"She's hardly spoken to me, Gwen…"

That was the truth, after all, I told myself.

"Well, if you talk with her again, tell her I would appreciate it if she would buy a piece of art rather than kidnapping my artists." Gwen was smiling, but I knew she was serious.

January 13, midnight

I didn't remember falling asleep after what seemed like hours of tossing and turning. A ringing sound woke me. Destiny. Will. One of them.

I stumbled to the door, but no one was waiting for me. The ringing persisted.

The phone, of course. I knew it was Paul.

He sounded eager and concerned on the other end of the line. His voice was soft, coddling me as I slipped into the plush armchair near the desk. I flipped on a light and listened. I pictured him slouched in the green beanbag chair, with all of his papers and documents strewn around the floor. He was running a hand through the curly hair that he had always hated but I had always loved.

"Kat, I've been going crazy over here thinking about you, worrying, wishing you were home."

"Oh, Paul, I've been meaning to call you… It's just that my head's been in the clouds, but things are going fine—really."

"What are people saying about the show?"

"Gwen says we're getting a lot of positive feedback. She's used to these kinds of things, so she knows better than I do." I stifled a yawn.

"I didn't want to wake you, but I haven't been able to reach you at any other time. I was getting desperate."

Why did his voice have to take on such a soothing,

melodious tone anyway?

We'd been together since college. Give or take three or four breakups. Oh, I tried to break free of Paul for good, but it never worked out. He'd betrayed me so many times, yet he always managed to smooth things over. Each time, I felt we had to give it one more half-hearted attempt.

I guess it was because I remembered how he left me love notes every day until I agreed to go out with him. He still was known to leave me little "I love yous" around the apartment. Then there were the surprise weekend trips and bundles of lovely flowers on my birthday. When I thought of those sorts of things, I got goopy-eyed and any sense of resolve disappeared. But how could all of this make up for the betrayal? That's what I had asked myself over and over. I never wanted to face the answer.

"Kat," he said, interrupting my thoughts, "when are you coming home? And I don't mean to New York, but back to our apartment. You can't stay with Blanche forever you know."

I had been living with my older sister ever since I had left the hospital. Paul and I were going through too much turmoil. At that point, there was no way I could return to what used to be our place. Yet, I did tell Paul that I would come back to him once I had finished with the show in London. Now, I silently cursed myself for the hasty words. I was scared. Frightened of my feelings for Paul, which returned in full force every time I heard his voice, and my secret longing for Will, who had been nothing more than an acquaintance in the dark.

"Kat, are you still there?"

"Yes, I am… Paul, I have work to do here."

"How about if I catch a flight over?" He must have been at the edge of the beanbag, set to head out the door.

"I'm not ready," I said, my heart pounding. "Paul, I have to take my time with everything. I'm still in recovery." There, I had said it. I had brought up the usual bone of contention. Paul was convinced that I never had been ill. That, he always said, isn't a real illness: You can control it after all! He didn't realize I continued to suffer in any way other than in my own imagination. But this time, he didn't fall into the trap.

"I know, Kat... I understand."

I swallowed hard and told him I would call soon and let him know the date of my return. It wouldn't be too far off, I said. Tears gathered in my eyes as I hung up the phone. But I didn't quite understand why.

January 15

I watched him climb into a cab, and it was too late. The car sped off as I called out his name. The pouring rain that drenched me in a matter of seconds drowned out my words. There wasn't another cab in sight. Nothing like New York. I couldn't even follow him.

I hurried inside. The guy at the front desk looked at me as if I were a madwoman dripping messily over the counter, but I didn't care.

"That man who got in the cab a minute ago... What room is he in?"

"We don't give out that kind of information, but in this case, it doesn't much matter. He's checked out."

"Checked out?" I felt as if a medicine ball had hit me in the stomach.

He nodded primly and then turned to chitchat with his haughty-browed colleagues.

It was over. Will was gone. Destiny said I would see him again, and I guess, technically, I had seen him. Tears filled my eyes. My emotions intimidated me. The room seemed to spin. I had to get out of here. I had to leave this hotel, with its strange nightly happenings and dreary, dim days that all ran together.

The first part of our exhibit would be over early next week. Gwen could handle it alone. She only acted as if she needed me to boost my pitiful sense of self. I ran blindly for the elevator. I had to pack, change tickets, do anything I could to leave and forget.

January 17

Finally, at home. Well, it wasn't really mine. It was Blanche's brownstone in the East Village, and that was about as close as I was going to get to any kind of home at this point. I curled up in the corner of the sofa and looked out the front window. Snow swirled from above. A few people waddled by in their heavy wool coats and leather boots. It almost seemed like daytime with the blanket of flakes reflecting light into the night sky. The steam of Earl Grey moistened my cheeks as I held the cup to my lips. Blanche knew everything now. She was my practical older sister and a tough corporate attorney—exactly the qualities that would make her the worst person to hear my story. But she listened and didn't tell me I was a complete lunatic. I guess she was happy because for the first time in a long while, I hadn't had a relapse. And I was able to eat a bowl of the chicken soup she brought home from the deli.

She studied me with her intense green eyes and deftly flipped her professionally straightened red hair over one shoulder. She held a pencil and a legal pad, as though still at work, even though it was 11 p.m. and both of us wore our flannel nightshirts. She jotted down notes as I spoke. She always did that when I had a problem, so I was used to it by now. She said it came with the business.

"It's a shame we don't have his last name," she said, tapping her pencil against the notebook. "Or his profession."

"That's all you can say about this whole fiasco, Blanche? I mean, what do you think of Destiny and those parties? Everything's in my imagination, right?"

"I didn't say that."

"You're thinking it though."

"Kat... that isn't true."

"How could it be real then? Explain it to me."

Blanche shook her head and took a sip of green tea.

"There could be a lot of explanations. Maybe those parties were in a different location that looks like the attic or whatever it was that you found. If Destiny spends a lot of time there, she's sure to know every inch of the hotel. She and her brother probably throw their parties secretly for a select crowd. That happens frequently in certain circles, Kat."

"I wouldn't know," I muttered.

"Don't sound so upset, Kat. I'm not out to destroy the magic of your experiences..."

She'd hit the nail on the head, but I wouldn't admit it.

"Get back to a normal life," Blanche said. "Write to Destiny asking for more information about Will. If she doesn't contact you, and that very well might be the case, then return to Paul or let him go forever." That was her solution to the problem.

"But what about those people I met?" I shook my head as I paced the room. "I can't forget about that fight between Destiny and Sam!"

"Kat, it's none of your business! You should be thinking of your recovery and future—not about other people's arguments."

I felt silly, of course, but too stubborn and curious to give in. I collapsed onto the couch and pulled my knees up to my chin.

My sister was still shaking her head as she took a final sip of tea. She asked me how long I planned to stay and if I was returning to my doctor. I replied, "I don't know" to the first question and "no" to the second.

She raised an eyebrow in the distrustful manner she'd been known for since we were kids. Then she asked if I was going to start looking for a job.

"I don't have to yet," I said. "That's the one thing going right so far—I've been paid for some of my work, so Gwen wants me to do a few more drawings for the second phase of the exhibit."

Blanche thought I had no artistic talent whatsoever, but she would never say so. She was too afraid it would drive me over the edge, but that kind of thing really didn't bother me.

"Kat, why don't you go back to the magazine?"

I closed my eyes and took a deep breath. Before my last ordeal, I had been a freelance writer for a lifestyle magazine. Then, I dropped out of sight. Better that than reveal the truth of my unsteady mind. I had ignored the messages and e-mails over the past few months.

"You're being completely irresponsible, you know," Blanche said, shaking her head. "How can you simply walk away like that? You enjoyed writing. Maybe it was the one thing that kept you going. And now, you're letting it slip away."

"Not completely," I snapped back. "I planned to contact Liz once... well once I get my life back in order."

"And she'll have forgotten about you by then, damn it!"

I swallowed hard, knowing she was right. But how could I explain everything that had been unfolding in my life?

"Does Paul know you're here?" Blanche asked.

"Not yet."

"So, what are you going to do?"

"I'm going to see him tomorrow." I said this almost as an order to myself. As if at least there was one situation I could handle.

March 1

I thought I would never pick up this journal again, but I was wrong.

I started dreaming of Will. I know it's him, yet I can't see his face clearly. I look at him through a haze in this place that's only familiar to me in my dreams—an ornate nineteenth century sitting room. Everything is pale pink. There's a marble fireplace against one wall with a big round mirror over it. The other walls are covered with portraits, but I can't see them clearly either. Heat from the fire warms my cheeks. I know this place doesn't exist. If it does, well... That's pretty worrisome because I've never seen it. Yet, I return here often when I'm in my deepest sleep. This is the first time Will is with me. I feel his soft mouth against my neck, his hands running down my back.

Then it's over, and I'm left sitting in the real world.

No word from Destiny. It was as if she had dropped off the face of the earth. I had returned to the tiny Soho apartment with Paul, and I was finishing up the final drawing for Gwen. It was for the recovery theme. She kept telling me I had to return for the second part of the exhibit, but I refused. I held these pages against my chest after re-reading what I had written. I hated myself for listening to Blanche. I should have known better. Every time I followed my sister's advice, I regretted it. Her advice led me back to the life I didn't want.

Paul slept soundly on our futon, unaware of my inner

turmoil. I touched the golden hair that curled across his forehead. He smiled and rolled over. I looked back at the pages I had neglected during these past few weeks and tried to summarize the situation.

I was eating somewhat normally again. I accompanied Paul to the movies or to dinner parties at friends' apartments. I visited Blanche once a week and called Mom in Connecticut. Everyone thought my life was going fine. Everyone except me. If things were normal, I wouldn't be haunted by thoughts of Will. I also wouldn't let whatever Paul said go over my head as I had been doing. I wouldn't feel as if I was living with a stranger. I couldn't help being angry at Destiny about all of this. She'd dragged me into this situation and then abandoned me. OK, maybe I had been naïve to play into her games. I should have shut the door right from the start.

March 17

"Why were you mumbling the name 'Will' in the middle of the night?" His voice was calm and steady as he stirred two sugars into his coffee. Feelings of guilt overwhelmed me. But I have no reason to be guilty, I told myself. My face reddened. The heat had become intolerable. I didn't know what to do or say. How could I possibly be honest? Paul would never believe my stories about the trip to London, and I wouldn't want to share them with him anyway.

"You've found someone else, haven't you?"

"What? You're being ridiculous..." I was grasping for words.

"Then who is Will?" he asked. A quiet accusation.

I wished I knew. But I wasn't going to say that to Paul, of course.

"I don't remember my dreams, Paul! What do you expect me to tell you?"

He took a sip of coffee and wandered over to the slim window in the corner of the kitchen. The fire escape partially blocked the view of busy early morning shoppers moving from one narrow storefront to the next.

"You're still angry, aren't you?" he asked.

"Well, I can't say I was thrilled that you cheated on me..."

"Kat, we were separated!"

"Yeah, I caught you in bed with our neighbor the day after we decided to cool it for a while. You didn't pick her up on the street corner five minutes earlier!" My words spewed out like a burst of lava from a volcano. "How am I supposed to deal with that? And the fact that this occurred right after I got out of the hospital… It was absolutely perfect!"

"Kat, I told you I regretted it! The only thing we can do now is come to terms with everything. I can't turn back the clock."

Sometimes, I wanted nothing more than to turn back the clock. Start again at zero, before the pain began. Have a second chance. But that didn't exist. Paul rushed over and pulled me into his arms. I pushed him away.

"There is someone else, isn't there?" he said, anger mounting in his voice. I wrenched my frustrated gaze from his fiery one. "It's about revenge, isn't it?"

I didn't think he really cared. The idea must have hurt his ego more than anything else.

"You weren't there when I was at my lowest, and now you think I have to answer your questions? I'm the one who has the right to be resentful—even after all this time!"

I felt the poisonous darts flying out of my eyes as raw emotions rose to the surface. I loved and hated him. I turned around and stalked across the living room. I had been crazy to return to him—to this place—when my feelings were tied into knots of confusion. I didn't belong here, going through the motions of normal life. It had to be all or nothing. And it couldn't be "all" until I let go of the memories, of the resentment.

"Where are you going?" he asked.

I pulled on my boots, and grabbed my handbag and wool coat in a matter of seconds. I didn't care that I was wearing my old jeans and my hair was escaping in frenzied tufts from its ponytail. I simply had to get out of there. An internal voice tried to convince me I was finally breaking free. Yet, deep down, I knew I wasn't.

"I need some air." I hated myself for not leaving forever.

Later that day

I could hardly believe my eyes. As I was walking out of the Union Square subway station, I found myself face-to-face with Sam. We both recognized each other at the same moment. I didn't know what to say, and he didn't either, so we said, "Hello, how's it going?" and other banal things. He had the same sad, worried look in his eyes that I remembered from the parties.

I asked him if he had a few minutes. We could run into a coffee shop around the corner... He said "yes," so we ordered two cappuccinos and settled down at a rather grimy booth in a place I had never noticed before.

"I've tried to reach Destiny, but she didn't answer my letter," I said. "I don't know how to get in touch with her..."

"You're better off this way, Katherine." His expression hardened.

"Why? I don't understand."

Sam took a slow sip of his drink and looked me directly in the eye. I could see the pain again.

"You can't put your faith in her," he said. "I did once, and I was wrong. She can't be trusted."

I shook my head. "Sam, this is all so vague..."

"I can't say much more," he murmured. "It's just that there are things Destiny could do or say to make a difference in people's lives. Yet, when it really matters, everything falls through. When it *truly* matters."

I swallowed hard. I was thinking of Will right at that moment. Was this the kind of scenario Sam was referring to? Bringing people together and then leaving them with no way of contacting each other?

"Isn't Gabriel her brother? What does he think of this?"

Sam closed his eyes and took a deep breath.

"We never could talk about Destiny," he said. "Gabriel would never admit that Destiny is responsible..."

"For what?"

"For what happened in my life, and in other people's lives. Like yours, for instance."

"You know something about Will?" I asked, leaning across the table.

Sam shook his head. "I don't think I know any more than you do. I saw him once, or maybe twice, at the parties. He's part of Destiny's past. Not part of her regular crowd. She probably wanted you two to meet because you belong together. It's as simple as that."

"Well then why didn't she give us a way to reach each other afterward?" I asked. I could hear the frustration in my own voice.

"As I said, Destiny only does part of the job. I'm tired of it, Katherine. I don't want to see her again, but I don't have a choice."

Sam's eyes were glassy with unshed tears. I reached across the table and took his hand. He smiled miserably and thanked me for my kindness.

"Why can't you tell Gabriel that you refuse to see his sister? If she's that much of a problem..."

"It's a complex situation, unfortunately. It's something I have to live with. But for you, Katherine, it's a different story. It's not too late for you to forget about Destiny, to break free!"

"She's my only link to Will," I said, almost to myself. I took a sip of my now cold coffee.

"That's the problem. It's a difficult choice."

"Well, for the moment, it looks as if I don't have one. She seems to have turned her back on me."

"Not for long," Sam said. "Believe me."

Sam's cell phone rang, and he picked it up. He had to leave. I asked for his number, and he scribbled it down on a napkin.

"One more thing," I said as he was slipping on his black trench coat. "How could it be that Destiny throws her parties in an attic that's under renovation?"

"Very simple," he said. "It's all an illusion."

He turned and hurried out the door before I could say anything further. Mouth half open, I sat there at the cracked wooden table and tried to understand the meaning of those final words. But it was impossible. Like everything else when it came to Destiny.

March 18

The scent of roses perfumes the pink sitting room in the late-afternoon sun. I'm laughing as he tells me stories of his trips to Paris and Rome. Will. It's him. I can feel it, yet I still can't see his face. Guiltlessly, I savor buttery cakes with raspberry jam. Then, I admire the thin gold bracelet he places on my wrist. A gift. His lips are against mine. My heart is racing.

Then a buzzing sound breaks into this magical moment.

I groaned as I rolled over and heard Paul mumbling about how he hated getting up early. Once again, we were giving our relationship another try. But these dreams haunting me almost every night weren't making things easy.

Sam's words resonated in my ears now and again: "It's all an illusion." What was that supposed to mean anyway? I had walked around the block a few times mulling the sentence over and over without reaching any kind of coherent conclusion. I yearned to know more, to understand. And then, as I was lingering at the foot of our building, Paul appeared at my side with a bouquet of flowers and apologies. He'd been looking for me everywhere, until finally he saw me wandering around Union Square like a lost soul. So he followed me... back here. I collapsed into his arms. One more reconciliation among how many? Maybe a hundred?

Now we faced each other a day later at the breakfast table. We shared a pot of coffee, and Paul opened a box of doughnuts. He handed me a sugar-coated one, and I pushed it away with distaste.

"It's happening again," he said.

"What do you mean?"

"Kat, you're hardly eating. You can't continue like this or you'll end up in the hospital again!"

"Paul, I'm fine."

But I knew he was right, and I was living on the edge. One more step and it—the anorexia—would be in control again. There, I said it. For the first time, that word entered my journal. It didn't scare me. It was hanging over my head, though, ready to deal a blow. There were days when I wouldn't eat. Then I realized the danger and forced myself to finish a meal. I wanted to starve myself, but I wouldn't. I refused to fall apart. Ironically enough, this diary was supposed to be about my illness in an attempt to pull me out of it, yet that hadn't been the case until these words. It had been in the background. Pushed there by Destiny, Will and everything that had been unfolding over the past several weeks. Maybe that was why I hadn't given in to the temptations of the illness that had been controlling my life for so long.

Paul shook his head and looked at me with desperate eyes.

"You're right," I said. "There are days when I fail, but I make up for them on the following day. This disease won't go away overnight. It's not my choice, Paul, even though you think it is!"

Tears streamed down my cheeks all of a sudden, and Paul held me close. For the first time in a long while, it felt good to be in his arms. This only made life more difficult.

April 1

And then one day the doorbell rang. The winter gloom was starting to melt into a brisk, but sunny, spring. I hurried through the beam of light stretching across the living room and unlatched the lock. My voice caught in my throat, my heartbeat accelerated, and I froze to the spot. Will. Smiling, he drew me in through the warmth of his eyes.

He took my trembling hand. I felt overheated. I couldn't speak as I led him inside. We were alone. His lips touched mine. The room seemed to be spinning. I pulled away. I couldn't be trapped a second time.

"I didn't think I would see you again," I finally said, my voice a whisper.

"So you didn't believe Destiny?"

"I don't understand her!"

"You're not alone, Kat."

"What kind of power does she have over us, Will? Who does she think she is anyway?"

"She doesn't have power over anyone. She has an ability—a rather unique ability that allows her to help people."

"Then why does Sam say the exact opposite? And why did she introduce us and then abandon the whole thing? She hasn't been helping me very much! Does she fool around with people's minds because she's a rich girl with nothing better to do?"

"No, she would never play around like that," Will said, his

expression turning solemn. "Sam's story is completely different. And tragic. Destiny and Sam should be the ones to tell you about it."

"How did you find me, Will? Or did you know where I was all along?" I took a step back and looked at him through narrowed eyes. I had difficulty trusting anyone, although deep in my heart, I knew he was sincere.

"Destiny helped me. She said the timing was right. But there's more. There's something you should know."

"What do you mean?"

"She's... seriously ill."

"What?" I couldn't believe my ears. That flamboyant, free-spirited young woman? The whole idea seemed preposterous.

Will nodded and bit his lip.

"What are you talking about, Will? And how serious is this?" My words were running together, and a sense of panic had overcome me.

Will took my hands again. I didn't pull away.

"It's terminal. An illness... a long-term illness. I don't know if she'll make it through this time. But she wants to see you, Kat. She has to see you before anything happens!"

"You expect me to pack up and fly to London?"

"I have two tickets here, one for you and one for me."

Thoughts raced through my mind. There wasn't any time to weigh the pros and cons or examine whether or not I was making the right decision. Will showed me the tickets. The flight was in a few hours. How could I explain this to Paul? I would scribble a note, saying Gwen needed me. It wasn't a complete lie. She was hoping I would return for the second part of the exhibit anyway.

April 1, late evening

Will Delaney. That was the name written on his ticket. I had taken a mental note of it, as well as the address on his luggage tag. He lived in New York. The Upper West Side. He might as well have resided in another state. Except for medical appointments, I didn't venture uptown very often. I preferred losing myself in the crowd downtown, with its grubby, narrow streets and colorful storefronts.

Will squeezed my hand as the plane lifted off, and I drew in a sharp breath.

"We'll be there before you know it," he said as if to reassure me.

I leaned against his shoulder and savored feelings of comfort and excitement. We remained that way for I don't know how long until finally a flurry of jumbled words rushed out of my mouth.

"Who are you, Will? We hardly know a thing about each other, yet I feel as if I've known you forever. And you never answered my question: Why did Destiny want us to meet?"

My heart was beating a mile a minute as his lips touched my cheek. He whispered into the curls that tumbled recklessly over my ears.

"I'm thirty-four, was born and raised in New York, and after some time wandering the globe, I finally decided to commit to something—my photography. I opened up a gallery a few years ago. Now I travel around looking for inspiration. I spent the past couple of months looking for you, but that isn't an easy task in New York. Then Destiny helped me out. And that about sums it up. As for your other question, it's best if Destiny explains everything. That's her responsibility. When she stirs something up, she has to be the one to follow through on it."

"And she doesn't always? Follow up, I mean."

"She tends to get distracted. That isn't the case this time, though."

He shook his head and sank into silence.

"What's going on with her, Will?"

"She has leukemia," he said. "She was diagnosed about three years ago, right after, well, after a rather personal family tragedy. It's been a constant struggle, but things have been going downhill over the past few months."

I was petrified. For this woman I hardly even knew, tears sprang into my eyes. Silently, I blinked them back. I wanted to know more, but didn't dare ask. It was as if, out of respect for Destiny, there was a certain barrier I couldn't cross.

"I saw your artwork in London," Will said a few minutes later.

I slid farther down in my seat.

"Yeah, pretty pathetic isn't it?" I said. "I'm not an artist."

"No, actually it's moving—a window into the soul."

"Well mine was pretty screwed up when I did that."

He squeezed my hand again, and I gazed out the window into the night sky.

"What happened, Kat?"

"It wasn't about food," I murmured, almost as if I were in a daze. "It never was, as a matter of fact. That's exactly why it became the focus of my attention. To push away the sadness I didn't want to exist. I don't know where this sadness came from, or what it was all about. Blanche—my sister—and I had a very ordinary childhood. And then I snapped. Mom thought it was because of the dieting shit that my friends talked about, but they weren't anorexic! Mom said I was vulnerable, so that's why I got sick and they didn't. But why was I vulnerable? No one could figure it out. That remains the mystery. So I have to live with it or die. And I haven't been very good at suicide."

I felt my face reddening and my heart racing again.

"I don't know why I'm telling you this. It's a lot more than you bargained for, I'm sure."

"No," he said, shaking his head. "I want to understand you. The truth doesn't frighten me."

"And you don't think I've suffered from an imaginary illness?" I asked, thinking of Paul.

"Of course not! Why would I?"

"Just wondering."

We remained silent for a moment, then I turned back to him.

"Why didn't you forget about me?" I asked. "There are plenty of women in New York."

"I haven't been able to get you out of my mind. It's as simple as that."

April 2

Will told me it would be best if I visited Destiny alone. He closed the cab door and told the driver to take me to her place in the lavish Kensington Square. She liked living there because she could stroll through Hyde Park during the day, and take a short cab ride to the theater almost every Friday and Saturday night, Will said.

My eyes followed my traveling partner as he dragged our bags into the lobby of The Grand East Hotel. The car jerked forward with a jolt and rolled away from the curb. Dizzily, I gazed at the colors and lights that shone through the hazy mist falling from the sky. I could feel my heart pounding double time.

What would I say to Destiny? How could I ask petty questions when she was fighting for her life? Right at that moment, I regretted this impulsive trip into no man's land. I hated the grim dark clouds, the damp, musty odor lingering in the air and the steady humming of the engine.

I wanted to go home. I felt nauseated as raindrops distorted the front stoops, the dark rooftops and the passersby hurrying along. What must have been Hyde Park was a long blur of trees, wilting under the pounding water. I don't know how much time had passed, but suddenly, the car rumbled to a halt in front of a rose-colored Victorian-style house. We were on a tiny tree-lined side street that seemed sheltered from the hustle and bustle of shops and restaurants. I pressed my credit card into the driver's hand, sloppily signed the receipt and bolted out the door.

So there I was, rushing up the four steps to the front door. Water clung to my hair and moistened my hands as they pressed the bell. A small, round woman opened the door almost immediately and ushered me into the vestibule. The space was dim but elegant, with golden wallpaper and vases overflowing with lilies.

"You must be the young lady who's come from the States?" the woman said. "I'm Margaret Bloome, the nurse."

She handed me a small business card with the words "Bloome Agency" inscribed on it. I smiled and introduced myself.

"I'm afraid you won't be able to see Destiny today," Margaret said. "She's much too tired, and we can't take the risk of getting her too excited."

"I won't cause any trouble," I said, desperate to see Destiny as soon as possible.

"Of course, I know you have the best intentions. But it wouldn't be a good idea. She's had visitors over the past few days, and I'm afraid they've drained her energy. I shall have our driver take you back to your hotel, and we'll call for you when Destiny is a wee bit stronger. Perhaps tomorrow will be a better day."

I looked at her pathetically, but I couldn't insist. I had no choice but to return to The Grand East Hotel.

☙❧

A half hour, maybe 40 minutes later, I stood in front of the same freckled-face attendant who, a couple of months earlier, had looked at me as if I were crazy. She slid a sealed envelope across the counter.

"The gentleman who checked in your baggage left this note for you," she said. "Your room is No. 406. Do you need assistance?"

"No, I can find it on my own," I said, wrinkling my brow in confusion. "That gentleman... Will Delaney... Can you tell me what room he's in? Since he checked in my suitcase, we're obviously not strangers."

"But he doesn't have a room here, Ma'am. He left straight away."

I looked at her blankly for a moment, thanked her in a dull voice, and gripping the envelope in one hand, hurried to the elevator. I felt tears of frustration in my eyes, but I wouldn't let them fall.

I stepped out at the fourth floor and followed the open corridor. I glanced into the atrium. Everything was still, silent. I didn't see one soul as I made my way through a doorway, turned left, then walked through another doorway, turned left again and finally spotted No. 406. A narrow glass table holding a vase of pink roses was the only spot of color in the hallway. After slipping my pass into the magnetic slit, I rushed into the room, half opening the envelope with one hand and rolling my suitcase with the other.

I didn't bother to examine this familiar place. With curtains drawn to block any natural light, all of the rooms wore the same dim shades of gray. I sank onto the down comforter and yanked a thick yellow notecard from the now-ragged envelope.

Dear Kat,

    The last thing I want to do is deceive you—please remember this as you read my words. I brought you here to see Destiny and to accept the things she has to reveal. I'm no longer needed here in London. Our future together is in New York. That's where I'll be, waiting for you. No matter how long it takes. You probably have a million questions, but believe me, it's better this way.

Will

I read the note over and over, as if somehow I would understand it more clearly after the fifth or sixth time. Feelings of elation and angry confusion collided, making a rather unpleasant cocktail.

"Damn it, Will!" I shouted, tossing his letter onto the bed and springing to my feet. I was tired of playing games, especially since I seemed to be the only one without a copy of the rulebook.

Waiting for you. The words made my heart soar.

But how could he be sincere when the only thing he seemed interested in doing was delivering me to Destiny? How could he return to New York so abruptly if he really was falling in love with me? Or was he? He never mentioned the word love. Maybe this was nothing more than a cruel game.

I closed my eyes and collapsed onto the bed. I thought of Paul, the good times and the bad. I thought of Will's lips on mine. Destiny. Gabriel's parties. Sam's sadness. Everything whirled together until those unwanted tears escaped, savoring their liberty.

April 3, after midnight

Long hallways led the way. I pushed open sets of fire doors and moved from modern to Victorian and back again. The staircases, antique with white scalloped edges, grandly led to a string quartet on one level and to darkness on another. I marched with purpose, as if desperately seeking someone or something. Alone as I climbed from one flight to the next, followed one sign to another. Only to find myself back to where I started. A complete loop. I turned around in frustration and had another shot at my search for nothing in particular.

Narrow bamboo steps led to an open platform. Books and magazines left behind on a few coffee tables. Drapes drawn in all of the rooms overlooking this plateau. Other than the rowdy crowds closed into the restaurants and the elegant couples enjoying classical music, the rest of the hotel remained masked in silence. It was as if I was the only person who dared to explore anything above the ground floor. I felt lost wandering those halls. I saw no one except my own reflection from time to time in a mirror that interrupted the sparseness of the white walls. The blue-gray carpet absorbed even the slightest sound of my footsteps.

An end table placed squarely against a wall—empty but for plastic fruit and two cocktail glasses left behind. By whom? Those revelers who congregated in one of the smoky bars or by Destiny's crowd? Silence. The air conditioners softly whirring. A door slamming now and again. Light footsteps scurrying. Then, nothing.

In a sudden panic, I turned and ran. I was afraid. I pushed open one fire door, then turned a corner. The wrong way. I couldn't be lost. No, I was just dazed. A sign for the elevator. A beacon of light. My feet pounded over the glass bridge leading to the atrium. I shuddered, my fear of heights taking over. And then I found safety as my fingers landed on the right button, whisking me down to the fourth floor.

I was tired. Exhausted wouldn't have been an exaggeration. But in spite of the densely soft down comforter and six feather pillows, I couldn't lay my soul to rest.

April 3

Margaret served muffins and Earl Grey in the drawing room. I held the pink porcelain cup between my hands as she opened the curtains to unveil a colorful rose garden. The previous day's rain had given way to misty sunlight.

"It's Destiny's pride and joy," Margaret said.

I nodded politely and glanced at my surroundings: A red velvet loveseat against the opposite wall and the matching sitting chairs (one of which I was occupying) were the only furnishings in the room, apart from a little silver tea table. Pale silver wallpaper covered the wall in front of me and a built-in bookcase covered the one behind me. The place reminded me of one of the rooms in the dollhouse I had as a child.

It was 9 a.m. I had rushed over after discovering a note under my door. A driver was out front, waiting to escort me to Destiny's home. I stumbled about the room in the terrycloth slippers inscribed with "GE" and pulled on jeans, a sweater and a cloche hat that calmed at least the top part of my untamed hair. I felt drunk after my wanderings in the wee hours.

"Destiny will be down in a moment," Margaret said, approaching the French doors that led into the hallway. I nodded. Impatience and nervousness weaved knots in my stomach.

Barely an instant after the nurse disappeared, Destiny's slim hand pushed open the door. She was thinner and paler

than she had been a few months ago, but even in her
weakened state, she seemed to glow. I stood up, awkwardly
stepped forward and reached out to her. She took my hands
and beamed with obvious delight.

"Katherine, I'm so glad you could come." Her voice was a
bit shallower than usual, but velvety just the same. "Please
forgive me for turning you away yesterday, but some days are
more difficult than others."

"No, no, don't worry," I insisted. "Will told me about
your illness and I... I'm sorry... I don't know what to say."

And I truly didn't know what to say. I sat there in a stupor
as Destiny adjusted her silky lavender robe and settled on the
loveseat. My discomfort didn't seem to offend her. She smiled
brilliantly, lifted a cup of tea to her lips and took a delicate sip.

"Perfect," she said. Then she turned her attention back to
me.

"You don't have to say anything in particular, Katherine.
It's not the end of the world. I've accepted it, and I'm dealing
with it day by day. Today is going to be a good one. I can feel
it. So I'm not going to think about illness!"

Her eyes were shining—almost deliriously.

"I didn't call you here to take pity on me, Katherine." She
took a deep breath and leaned forward as if she had many
secrets to share. I noticed the dark circles under her eyes and
fine lines that fanned out from the corners. The weakness,
fatigue and medication had left their marks.

"I simply wanted to tell you a story, a true story," she said.
She placed her cup on its saucer and looked me directly in the
eye. "Now the question is: Are you ready to hear it?"

I nodded mechanically. I didn't understand what this was
about, but if her story would bring me any closer to a point of
clarity, I wanted to hear it.

"I've been gathering elements that relate to this story for a
very long time," she began. "The essential is there, but I don't
have every detail. That would be impossible. Let's start at the
beginning...

"Imagine a grand mansion right here in London. It was in
the 1880s. A young woman named Victoria lived there with
her husband Jonathan, whose family had made a fortune in tea

or something of the like. They were very much in love, and it showed. Most people would find such a couple quite charming. But not everyone, unfortunately. Jonathan's older brother was this exception. I'm not sure of his name, but the name Edward has come to me over and over again… Yes, I'm almost certain that's it.

"Jonathan and Edward were in business, so would often travel together. Victoria had two main weaknesses: She was terribly jealous and extremely proud. She imagined all of the young women who undoubtedly could tempt her husband when he was far from home. Edward decided to use her faults to his advantage. He dreamt of nothing but seducing her and breaking up his brother's marriage. And then, one day, he had an idea. Edward dragged Victoria to a brothel in a part of London she would never frequent. Right there, early in the morning, she saw her husband sneaking out of that horrid place!

"So the proud Victoria ceded to Edward's advances. A revenge that turned to despair when she learned some time later that Jonathan had only been looking for Edward at the brothel that morning…"

I gazed at Destiny with rapt attention. I didn't know why she was telling me this. But it was a fascinating story—especially with Destiny as the narrator. Her melodious voice coaxed even the most reticent listener into her world. Through her words, I felt as if I had traveled back in time.

"Jonathan, of course, was furious at Victoria for having suspected him of such a thing and for taking revenge," Destiny continued. "Victoria, with her pride, couldn't live with herself. And so she didn't. Jonathan found her in the attic…"

Tears welled up behind my eyes. Sure, it was the kind of tale that would naturally stir up one's emotions, but this time, it was more than that. My own wounds were too fresh. Any story of suicide was enough to bring up too many memories. Destiny handed me a tissue.

"Are you all right?" she asked. "I tried to keep the details to a minimum, Katherine. I didn't want to upset you any more than necessary."

"No, that's OK, I'm fine. The whole thing is so tragic

though. I have trouble dealing with tragedy." The lump in my throat wouldn't go away. I tried to choke back tears as I dabbed at my eyes.

She nodded and remained silent.

"It's an interesting story, Destiny," I whispered. I couldn't explain the real reason for my chagrin. I didn't want to go into that ordeal. It was still too painful.

"There's a reason why I told you this, Katherine. It's not easy to accept, of course, but there isn't any other way of breaking this to you. I called you here because now you can make things right again."

"Me? But what do I have to do with them?"

I shuddered. She couldn't possibly be referring to my suicide attempts.

"Katherine, you *were* Victoria."

I stared at her for what seemed like forever. Silence. Everything was in slow motion. She turned to cough, then turned back and smiled. It was one of those kind, compassionate expressions that invite the sharing of secrets. I didn't know what to think or feel. Had she completely lost her mind? Exactly what kind of horrible game was she playing? Were Destiny and Will both out to drive me crazy?

But I had to keep calm. I couldn't yell at a woman who was terminally ill. A few stray tears slipped down my cheeks.

"Destiny, I think it's best if I go… I don't want to be part of… of this story. It doesn't make sense. I think you have the wrong person."

Destiny gently touched my arm.

"Katherine, I told you this wouldn't be easy, but we don't have much choice in the matter. I know this is painful. It reminds you of your suicide attempts, the years of physical and mental suffering, the battle with anorexia. You never understood the reason for your misery. Life at home was perfectly normal—or at least as normal as everyone else's! Your sister Blanche led a charmed existence while you fought invisible demons."

The tears continued to fall. How did she know all of this about me? I felt sick to my stomach. I wished I never had come here. Will must have known what was going on. How could he have led me here? For once, I wanted to be back at home with Paul. I never should have agreed to come to London and The Grand East Hotel in the first place. Why hadn't I been able to accept my life as it was?

"Paul isn't meant for you," Destiny said. "This is your last chance to be with your one true love! Don't throw it away, Katherine!"

"What are you talking about? And how do you know about Paul and Blanche... and everything? This is too crazy."

I got up and stumbled forward. Coughing, Destiny rose from the loveseat and grabbed hold of my arm.

"I can tell you things about your past and your future, and as you can see, they're true." For the first time, Destiny's voice took on a sense of urgency. "You have to go to Will. Don't be angry with him. You can't hurt him again! You can't hurt yourself again."

"What do you mean about Will?" I asked.

Destiny continued coughing. She gripped my arm, as if for support. Before I could help her back to the couch, Margaret came rushing into the room.

"Destiny, you know you're not supposed to be doing this! To be getting all excited!" She shook her head, put a firm arm around Destiny and nearly dragged her toward the French doors. "She goes into a coughing fit every time she gets upset."

"Wait!" Destiny said between coughs as she pushed Margaret away with one burst of violent energy. She looked at me then with wide eyes. "Will was Jonathan! He knows this and has for a long time. He's been working with me and searching for you."

"Destiny, this is outrageous! I can't believe any of it. How can you expect me to fall for such a joke?"

The coughing again. Margaret yanked Destiny back toward the door and looked at me in annoyance.

"Can't you see she should not be disturbed? Really! Whether you agree with what she has to say or not, can't you let the poor girl be? She's probably hallucinating. I'm taking her up to bed. The driver is out front to take you back to the hotel."

I felt as if I had been slapped. Margaret was right, but I was too shaken to be using any judgment. I had to get out of there.

"Katherine, all I ask is that you think this over before saying you don't believe." Destiny's voice rang out as the nurse helped her up the stairs. "Think of what you've seen and heard over the past few months. Do you really need more proof?"

April 3, late evening

I had cried myself dry. Salt-stained cheeks, puffy eyes and a stack of rumpled tissues were testimony to what I had been doing since I left Destiny's house. Thoughts raced through my head. I struggled to analyze the situation.

Was this some kind of dumb joke? Or was insanity involved? The first scenario seemed highly unlikely. Destiny wouldn't put herself through so much trouble over a period of months to fool some stranger. It wasn't as if she or anyone else would have much to gain from it.

Craziness could be an explanation. What if, slowly but surely, Destiny was losing her mind? She was suffering from a serious illness after all. But that didn't explain Will's role or the fact that Destiny seemed to have a window into my soul. My mother, Blanche and Dr. Bell were the only ones who knew the details of my life and the mental turmoil that had sprung up out of nowhere.

There was only one option I couldn't accept or even consider: the idea that everything Destiny had said was true. The real world wasn't a place for fairytales, time travel and magic wands. I wasn't a 5-year-old, and I wasn't about to be treated like one. Destiny, by somehow throwing me some accurate information about myself, was expecting me to swallow an absolutely impossible story along with it.

These thoughts twisted themselves through my mind as I tossed and turned in the darkened room. I wanted the night to be over. The next morning, I would hurry to the airport with my return ticket and try to get on the next flight to New York. I would return to Paul and a somewhat normal life. And I would forget about everything that had unfolded at The Grand East Hotel over the past few months. With all my might, I would push away any and every thought of Will. He was part of this web of madness and nothing more.

∞∞

Someone shaking me. Waking me up. I peered groggily out of bleary eyes.

"Katherine! We're going to be late!"

Destiny's voice.

She grabbed my hand and led me to the door. I stumbled after her. Trying to organize thoughts in my dazed mind. What had happened yesterday? Had it been a dream? No, wait a minute. Was this a dream? Destiny was supposed to be ill, weakened. Yet she stood before me with glowing eyes and a bright smile. She wore a pink, billowy dress that almost matched the color of her cheeks.

Before I could resist, we were in the hallway and she was leading me to the place that had become so familiar.

"I thought you were sick?" I called out after her.

"I told you this was going to be a good day!"

"But earlier, you were coughing."

"Oh, that's when I get too excited about something," she said with a wave of her hand. "No worries. It's nothing!"

"How do you know so much about me?" I asked.

"Then you do believe me."

"I didn't say that."

Destiny grinned.

"Katherine, it's either all or nothing. Once you're willing to accept the whole truth, we can talk about it. Until then, you're not ready."

I furrowed my brow as I hurried after her.

"What if I said I believed you?"

"Now *I* don't believe *you*! I've dealt with enough cases like you, my dear Katherine. I'll know when you're sincere." She laughed lightheartedly and led me up the ladder to our usual spot behind the bar.

The party was in full swing as we rose to our feet and stepped around the counter. The bartender handed us each a glass of champagne. I held mine gingerly between shaky hands. Destiny took a sip of hers, set it down on the counter and scanned the room. Wall-to-wall people. The disco balls reflected beaded dresses, tuxedo shirts and well-shined shoes. They danced to disco this time. *Dancing Queen.* A young woman wearing a sequined miniskirt stood on a makeshift stage with the band and shimmied to the music.

Although everyone appeared to be ignoring my disheveled appearance, I still felt uncomfortable standing there in bare feet and a nightgown. This is becoming a habit, I thought to myself, wryly.

Suddenly, the girl with the sequined miniskirt was no longer with the band and instead was greeting Destiny with a kiss on both cheeks. She had a round porcelain-doll face, accentuated by large blue eyes.

"Katherine, this is my best friend Audrey," Destiny said.

Audrey kissed me on the cheek and flashed a perfect smile.

"I hope you enjoy the party," she said. Then she turned to Destiny.

"I didn't know you were going to be able to make it."

"When there's a will, there's a way," Destiny said. "I think you should return to the band. They can't go on without you."

Audrey laughed and hurried away with more ease in her stiletto heels than most people in sneakers. Destiny had turned away from the musicians and was scanning the rest of the room.

"Who are you looking for?" I asked. "Why did you bring me here this time? Will's left, you know. There's no point in trying to find him here."

"If you want to see Will, you no longer need me, Katherine," she said, smiling. "I've done my part. At this point, it's up to you."

Before I could say another word, someone called my name. Sam. He left Gabriel talking with someone near one of the windows and was making his way in our direction.

"Poor Sam," Destiny said, shaking her head. "Why can't he learn to accept things the way they are and enjoy?"

"What do you mean?"

"Nothing. I'll leave the two of you to talk while I visit with my brother. Sam and I don't mix very well."

"But I still don't understand why you brought me here."

She either didn't hear my words or chose not to address the subject.

"Don't expect answers from her," Sam said after kissing me on the cheek. "How've you been?"

"Not that well—mentally, I mean."

"I'm glad I ran into you," Sam said. "Listen, you have to get out of this place. Go home to New York and don't come back. That's what I've been trying to do, but unsuccessfully. It's not too late for you to return to a normal life! What's so great about these parties anyway? Surrounded by a bunch of bombastic fools who try to convince themselves that this is living…"

"Sam, I want to understand what this is all about! That's what's kept me coming back for more! Before Destiny dragged me back here, I was dead set on leaving first thing in the morning. But, my curiosity is starting to win over."

"You need to leave this party if you hope to have any clear thoughts. C'mon, follow me."

Sam took my hand, and in a matter of minutes, we were down the ladder, across the hall and running backwards through the maze.

I woke up with a start and threw back the comforter.

"Sam!" I cried out. "Sam! Where are you?"

I looked around in confusion. From what I could remember, we had been running through the halls together. That was it. The next thing I knew, I was sitting at the edge of the bed and narrowing my eyes to see 7:05 flashing on the alarm clock.

"Shit!"

I marched into the bathroom and stepped into a hot shower. As the droplets drummed against my back, I closed my eyes and went over the details of the previous night. Everything was extremely clear. It couldn't have been a dream. This was yet another one of the bizarre experiences linked to both Destiny and this hotel.

I thought back to our visit in her living room and then pushed it away. Nonsense. The whole story was a lot of baloney. If I kept thinking about it, I would start crying again. My problem was that whenever there was a question, I had to find an answer. Maybe there weren't always answers, and maybe I had to face that. Maybe I would never understand how Destiny had gotten that information about me.

I wrapped myself in a terrycloth robe and opened the door to grab the newspaper. If I wanted to return to a normal life, my best option would be to forget everything and go home. Follow Sam's advice. But I couldn't. I was my own worst enemy, and I knew it.

I flipped through the newspaper until a tiny headline in the lower right corner of the real estate section caught my eye.

The Grand East, Mysteries for Sale.

My eyes scanned the three-paragraph article that followed. An investor in the hotel was ready to cede a majority stake. The agency representing the property declined to name the owner or offer a reason for the sale. A quote from another real estate agent—likely bitter after losing out on the account—and the sentence that followed were what interested me the most.

"With all of the mysterious goings-on in that establishment, this might be a difficult sell," the agent said. "It's one of those secrets no one talks about, but everyone understands."

Indeed, hotel guests have complained about late-night music from the top floors and hushed whispers in the hallways. A hotel spokesman who declined to be identified said the only parties ever held are in the ballroom on the ground floor.

With the paper still in my hands, I sank onto the corner of the bed. Maybe there was more to this story than I had initially thought.

April 4, an hour later

"What's happened here?" I asked.

Gwen turned around, her face brightening. She was arranging some papers in the makeshift office we had used since the beginning.

"Kat, you've returned! As I had hoped—and right on time! The second part of this exhibit is going to be fabulous. Who knows? It could even be better than the first. Can you believe how much we've sold already?"

I hadn't paid any attention to the tally. After cashing the first few checks, I panicked. The unopened envelopes stacked up on my desk at home. Paul kept asking why I wouldn't open them, and I kept saying I was scared to see my failure. Then he would roll his eyes, shake his head and mumble something about how arguing with me was pointless.

Gwen kissed me on both cheeks and nearly pushed me into one of the angular armchairs she had acquired since my departure. She was saying something about how successful we'd been so far, but I was too preoccupied to join in on the excitement.

Finally, I pressed the newspaper into her hands.

"Gwen, read this. And then tell me what you really know about this place and about Destiny."

Her glowing eyes dimmed, and she gazed at me curiously.

"Go ahead," I said. "It's pretty short."

She scanned the lines and then looked up.

"Why are you asking me, Kat?"

"Because you've held other exhibits here, Gwen… and you know pretty much everyone who comes through these doors. You've heard things."

Gwen sank back into her seat and sighed.

"Gossip isn't always the way to go, Kat. I hear many, many stories, but you can only believe about one percent of them."

"I'm interested in the strange happenings in this place. I'm not the only one who's witnessed them!"

Gwen was silent for a moment, and I could almost see the wheels turning in her mind.

"Yes, you're right. I've had some experiences myself."

"Destiny came to your door too?"

She shook her head.

"No, I've heard the late night parties, the laughter. And then when I checked around, I never saw a thing."

"And in spite of that, you keep coming back?"

"Why not?" she asked, shrugging. "What difference does it make? Perhaps it even adds a bit of charm to this otherwise very proper hotel."

"You don't want to get to the bottom of it? You have no desire to find out why?"

"Kat, I'll leave that to the detectives and so should you. There's a reasonable explanation for everything. It's nothing to get excited about."

"Well, apparently this could keep the hotel from selling!"

"That shouldn't matter to you."

"None of this would matter to me if I hadn't been dragged into it by Destiny!"

"What are you talking about, Kat?"

"Nothing. Never mind…" I was pretty frustrated at this point. "I only was hoping you might have some more information on the strangeness around here…"

"Kat, the mysterious party sounds have been going on for three years, and I think that's one of the reasons the owner wants to sell. The hotel has lost some business because of the gossip, the stories and the noise. But some say the hotel has gained new visitors who are intrigued. So who knows if the reason is completely financial? Perhaps it's emotional as well. Now this article says the mystery factor could make it a hard sell. I suppose that's another perspective. Anyway, there's nothing more I can tell you. I think you have more of a privileged relationship with Destiny than I do."

"Why do you say that?"

"Because she comes to see you. Why don't you ask her your questions? She's the one with the answers about the parties and things, isn't she?"

"Yeah, but the problem is she doesn't share them."

"My turn now: I have a question for you." Gwen stood up and took a step toward me. "Have you returned to take part in this exhibit or are you going to disappear again?"

"I can't stay here, Gwen. I have to go home... to start over."

"That's not easy."

She wished me luck as I took the newspaper and hurried out of the room.

April 10

I doodled on the first page of my empty notebook. A few flowers and raindrops. As if that would take my mind off the task at hand. What else to do in a waiting room wallpapered with glossy photographs of castles, vineyards and cocktail parties? I had already flipped through the latest magazine issue featuring spa getaways and tossed it back on the coffee table. I exchanged awkward glances with the new receptionist and then turned my attention to the pages that would soon be filled with my rapid drawings.

Once again, I had followed Blanche's advice. I sketched her face, with that authoritative expression I knew too well. So there I was, nervously waiting for Liz to appear at the door and lead me through the familiar newsroom. I hardly had enough for any kind of decent story pitch, but I would figure something out. What choice did I have? Sure, I had finally opened the envelopes from Gwen to discover checks adding up to a couple thousand dollars. But I couldn't live on that. I refused to rely on Paul or my sister or anyone else for that matter.

Paul. I drew the annoyed expression that often looked back at me. Disapproval was surrounding me lately. And I had only returned to New York five days ago. Oh, I guess you could say things fell into place easily enough. Paul welcomed me with open arms. I settled back into our apartment and not a word was mentioned about the real reason behind my absence. I hadn't sought out Will, and he hadn't appeared at our doorstep either. No word from Sam. No word from Destiny. No word from Gwen.

"Kat, how are you?" With her silver bob bouncing gracefully, Liz rushed into the room and took my hands. "Come on in. Sorry, I'm running late as usual!"

As I followed her, I nodded at those who maybe vaguely remembered me from better days. Back copies of the magazine, various newspapers, notebooks and gym bags littered the desks and floor. A recorded version of the latest Academy Awards show was playing on the flat screen along the far wall, and most eyes were turned in that direction.

I sank into the beanbag chair facing Liz's desk and took a deep breath.

"I shouldn't have dropped out of sight like I did," I said. "I had some health issues to deal with."

"Kat, I know," she said in her most discreet voice. "We saw how thin you had become."

I felt my face go hot. Had I truly thought I could hide my problem? I mean, going from 130 pounds to 85 isn't something people don't notice. The thought only occurred to me now, making me feel silly. I looked down and tried to regain my composure.

"You don't owe me an explanation," Liz continued. "I'm simply glad to see that you're doing well. So, let's get down to business. You have a story idea, I suppose?"

"Yes, and no... I mean... It's complicated." I felt flustered, but my voice took over where my courage faltered. "I was staying at this rather odd hotel in London this winter and observed a few strange happenings—noises in the hallway, unexplained laughter coming from nowhere. There's this woman named Destiny who has these fancy parties and spends a lot of time around the hotel—but during the night. Now the place is for sale, and they say it's going to be difficult. Apparently, I'm not the only one who's noticed something unusual."

I handed her a copy of the newspaper article.

Liz read it and looked at me over the rim of her rimless

glasses. Then she took them off and placed them on her desk as she usually did when she had to mull over a problem.

"I like the idea, Kat, but there isn't enough meat to it. Maybe it would be something to monitor and come back to if and when they find a buyer. I'm sure the new owner would make some changes, so we could have a snazzy piece on what's being done. Some before and after shots, perhaps? We'll have to think about it…"

"But the mystery behind it is the most interesting element, Liz! I'm sure I could find guests to interview about what they've seen and heard… and Destiny's parties…"

"That should be part of it, of course, but we don't have enough for the moment, Kat. Our issues have been so full lately that only an outstanding story would be reason to bump something we already have planned. I'm sorry."

I nodded, trying to hide the disappointment of defeat.

"Let's talk again soon," Liz said, leaning forward and patting my arm. "I might have a few short pieces you could take on if that interests you."

I nodded again.

"Call me in about a month, then." She flashed a wide smile that did nothing to soften the rejection that had smashed my spirits.

I thanked her and slipped out of the newsroom before anyone could stop me for an unwelcome chat.

April 10, 6 p.m.

"She wasn't interested," I said, glancing at my sister out of the corner of my eye. Blanche had convinced me to join her at a bar near her uptown office for a drink. Through the dusty windowpane, I studied the passersby carrying briefcases and coffee cups. Women who had exchanged their heels for sneakers rushed down steps to the subway station.

"Kat, are you listening to me?"

"Hmm?"

Blanche wore her annoyed look once again.

"Kat, I was saying that it's probably for the best your editor didn't accept the idea. The good news is she wants you to work on some other projects. I think you need to put everything that's happened over the past few months behind you. I'm concerned about you! Granted, for the first time, you seem to be breaking free from the eating disorder. I suppose that's the most important thing. I actually am astonished and impressed to see how your focus has completely changed. In the past, you were never able to move forward so quickly. I should accept that and be grateful, but I can't help being bothered by something else... I'm afraid that problem is being replaced by another. By another obsession of sorts."

I swirled the straw around in my glass of diet Coke and furrowed my brow.

"What are you talking about, Blanche?"

"The whole idea of contacting the magazine was to start

anew! You have to face reality, Kat. Either stay with Paul or dump him. But don't get involved in this fantasy world that you've discovered or created with those people you met in London!"

"It's not a fantasy world!" I felt like a defensive 12-year-old, but I didn't care. "Blanche, so far every time I've followed your advice I've fallen flat on my ass! I went back to Paul and tried to forget about everything. The situation with Paul didn't improve. And then... Let's just say the London experiences intensified."

I couldn't tell her about how Will had whisked me back to London or how Destiny had pleaded with me to believe her unbelievable story. Blanche would be on her cell phone to have me committed within the next 10 minutes. For the first time in my life, I couldn't share 100 percent of the story with my sister.

Blanche shook her head and took a sip of her martini. I only wished the drink would have a calming effect on her. I curled up in the bucket seat and set my glass on the table separating us.

"Look, Kat, there's a reason I'm adamant about you getting your life back together right away. I've always been here watching your every move, making sure everything was all right. But things are going to change soon."

"What do you mean?"

"I have an opportunity with the firm. A big business deal in Japan."

"You're going to Japan? For how long?"

"That's the thing, Kat... The plan is I'll move there for two years, which probably means it will turn out to be three years."

"Move?"

I tried to swallow the lump that had formed in my throat. I hadn't been prepared for this. As much as I complained about my sister, I was used to the sense of mental security she provided. We had never been separated for more than a few months.

She took my hand and leaned closer to me.

"Kat, don't be upset. Then I'll start crying and regret my

decision."

"I'm not."

"Be honest."

"Why didn't you tell me sooner?"

"I was afraid of your reaction. Your progress has been so great that my one fear was to put that in jeopardy. But of course it was silly of me. I knew I would have to tell you eventually."

Blanche shook her head. She wasn't used to making silly decisions.

"When are you leaving?" I asked, my voice no more than a whisper.

"In a month."

"Will you be ready by then?"

"Kat, the question is: Will you be ready? I want to have some assurance…"

I blinked to hold back the tears. I felt ridiculous for being such an emotional wimp. The anger toward my sister had evaporated. She was the only one I could really open up to after all. At least about most subjects.

"I'll be fine, Blanche."

"Promise me you'll forget about Destiny and that whole group."

"OK," I said. But it was a lie.

April 12

I woke up in a cold sweat. Crying. I had to put the pieces together, to reach into my memory. Those images far away, yet close all the same. I clenched the sheet in my hands, squeezed my eyes shut and tried to ignore Paul's even breathing beside me. I had been running through dim, empty cobblestone streets on the heels of a smartly dressed young man. I hadn't been able to see his face. I was tripping in my heavy shoes and long cloak, but he called out to me in annoyance. "Hurry along now!" I could still hear the words over and over in my head, but the sound of his voice had disappeared.

I tried to remain calm, to concentrate, hoping to remember the rest of the dream that had haunted me two nights in a row. I was certain Will had been a part of it, yet I couldn't call up a single scene involving him. I was struggling. It was too late. The dream's last traces had slipped away.

April 13

Paul held my hand across the table at the busy French brasserie and only let it go when the waiter delivered his *steak frites* and my grilled salmon. He was in his charming phase. For some reason, he had decided he would do anything to save our relationship—even if it meant accepting that I had been suffering from a real illness and everything had been pretty difficult for me over the past few years.

"Why are you doing this?" I asked.

"Doing what?" he replied, distracted as he chewed on a fry and cut into the rare meat.

"What I mean is… this talk about starting over, being the perfect couple. You think we have what it takes?"

"I did a lot of thinking while you were away," he said, setting down his fork and taking my hand once again. "I was a real asshole in the past. I've changed."

"What prompted the change?" I asked, studying him almost suspiciously. I twirled my fork in the rice, breaking down the fancy pyramid.

"Hearing you mumbling the name 'Will' in the middle of the night. Either you're having an affair with this guy or he's someone from your past."

I felt my face turn red, but Paul didn't seem to notice.

"Anyway, I realized that if you did cheat on me, I probably deserved it after the way I've behaved. It's been a wake-up call. And I was pretty miserable when you were away.

I don't want to lose you again."

"I'm not cheating on you."

"I know," he murmured. "You're above that kind of thing."

And for the first time in a long while, things were OK. We chatted about books and movies, and new restaurants in the city. As we strolled home in the brisk spring air, we marveled over the night sky and connected the stars to form constellations. We were on our best behavior as if it was a first date. Trying to convince ourselves that we could turn back the clock.

Two glasses of wine were enough to go to my head. Paul undressed me, and we tumbled onto the sheets.

April 30

Just when the dust seemed to settle, something came along to whip it up once again. Or I should say "someone."

I felt his presence before he said a word. Fumbling with my keys after locking the front door, I turned around, almost knowing he would be there.

"You look as if you were expecting me," Will said, taking a step closer. "That's a good sign."

"What are you doing here?" I asked, trying to keep my voice cool.

"Hmm, you don't sound as happy to see me as I'd hoped."

I took a deep breath and steeled myself against the desire that surged forth with such intensity. I would remain in control.

I tucked an untamed curl behind my ear, dropped the keys into my favorite straw bag and started walking. Will followed, putting his hand on my arm. An electric shock ran up my back. I stopped and turned to him.

"Why are you doing this? How did you and Destiny find out so much about my past? And why create the ridiculous fable about some kind of life together a century ago. You expected me to believe that?"

"You aren't tempted to entertain the idea? Even with the supporting evidence Destiny provided?"

"I don't see any kind of proof."

"If Destiny didn't have a special ability, how could she have known things about your childhood?"

"People have their ways of spying on others…"

"And why would Destiny lie to you anyway? Why would she create such a story?"

"That's what I'd like to know!"

"Listen, I understand. It's difficult to believe. I know it sounds preposterous. But haven't you ever heard of listening to your heart rather than following the common path?"

Will took my hands and pulled me closer as if we were alone in the world instead of on a street with dozens of passersby who couldn't care less about us anyway. My heart was pounding wildly. His mouth touched mine, lingering, delicate. Then passionately melting into my own. Right that second, I wished and hoped that Destiny's story could be true.

And then I took a step back. Back to reality.

"Show me some real evidence, Will," I said between gritted teeth. "All I've seen so far is smoke and mirrors."

I turned away from the sadness in his eyes and ran. As fast as I could, I zigzagged around couples, kids, strollers and street signs until I was far enough to let the tears run free.

I slammed the door and threw the newspaper (turned to the "help wanted" section) onto the floor along with the apartment keys. My heart raced as I stumbled into the darkness of the living room and followed a single light in the hallway. His brother's SUV was double parked along the curb and a pile of Paul's books and CDs filled the front seat.

"Paul!" I called out, hurrying into the bedroom. "What's going on?"

But I knew exactly what was happening even before he snapped the suitcase shut. He was leaving.

"I thought you were above that kind of thing," he said. "That's what I told you the other night, remember?"

He stepped toward me and grabbed my wrists.

"Stop it! You're hurting me!" I twisted my hands from his grasp and backed away. "What are you talking about anyway?"

"Oh, come on, Kat! Why don't we stop hiding things? Be honest and tell me you were kissing your lover Will right in front of our apartment. John and I saw the whole show!"

I trembled with the fear and embarrassment of being caught. He saw. He knew.

"Great to be walking down the street with a colleague and then see your girlfriend making out with another guy."

He glared at me through eyes filled with tainted pride.

"So that's what upset you the most then," I said. "Being embarrassed in front of a friend."

"Don't try to push guilt back to me, Kat!" He grasped my shoulders and wouldn't let go. "Your game won't work this time. I would have forgiven you if this was a story from the past, when things weren't going well between us. But we agreed to move on—together, truthfully. I trusted you! That it was over…"

"I trusted you once too," I said coldly, as he pushed me away and caught the handle of his suitcase.

Tears welled up in the corners of my eyes, but I wouldn't let them fall. They were tears of emptiness, of a total lack of emotion. I didn't care if he left or stayed. And I didn't even care that his ego was hurt more than his heart. For one split second, everything was meaningless.

I followed him into the living room and pointed to a pile of his business papers that remained in a constant clutter on the desk.

"Take all of your shit and get the hell out of here."

I felt liberated. This was the right decision. A clean break. Finally, an attempt to take charge of my life.

He glared at me as he scooped up every last one.

"Who is he, anyway, this Will? Someone you met in London while you were dodging my phone calls?"

"I think you should leave now." I inhaled and exhaled slowly as if somehow this relaxation method could transport me above and beyond.

He opened his mouth as if to say something, then obviously thought better of it, and made his way to the door. I didn't start breathing normally until the engine roared down the street.

৵৵

"Why did you do it, Kat?" Blanche asked, all reason an hour later as we sat facing each other on her couch.

I couldn't stay in the apartment I had shared with Paul. I wanted to erase the memories—good and bad. Blanche said that was nonsense. As usual, we never agreed.

"You mean break up with him or kiss Will in the middle of the street?" I asked.

"Both."

She handed me a cup of mint tea and took a sip of her own.

I stared into the yellowish liquid that drew me into a trance.

"Well?"

"The part with Will wasn't my fault. He started it, and then I pulled away. As for the breakup, it's the right thing, Blanche. I should have done it earlier instead of trying to patch up a relationship that has too many holes. I'm not sad about it—really."

"What's bothering you then? Something is there... weighing on your heart."

I couldn't tell her that what upset me the most was knowing that a strange force was pushing me in Will's direction. I was frightened. Of the story that was senseless. Of Destiny and her power. Of Sam and his sadness. And more than anything, I was afraid of what I was discovering within my own heart.

May 1

Blanche criticized me for my indifference.

"How could you toss away a long-term relationship without the slightest feeling one way or the other?" she asked as she piled papers into her briefcase.

I shrugged and stirred fake sugar into my coffee.

"And you're still not eating much, Kat," she said, shaking her head. "I'm worried about you. Damn it. You know I have to leave for this deal, and now I'm starting to wonder if I should cancel everything."

I jumped up with a start and took her hand.

"No. That's ridiculous! I can handle the situation. You're not my mother. Don't start treating me like a two-year-old again, Blanche. I knew I shouldn't have come here."

"You needed to come here. You needed me. What are you going to do in a few days when I'm gone?"

"Finish growing up," I said with a smirk.

"That's not funny, Kat."

"Look, don't you feel better knowing I'm not totally brokenhearted over Paul?"

"What if you're fooling yourself?"

"Blanche, let me worry about it."

"You're still thinking about Will aren't you? That's what this is really about, isn't it?"

"What makes you say that? I told you I pushed him away."

"But you didn't want to push him away!"

I tried to lower my gaze, but was trapped within the truth of her words.

"What does it matter anyway?"

"Kat, you're emotionally fragile, and I don't think he understands that." Her eyes wouldn't let mine escape. "This isn't the right time to begin an adventure with someone—especially after those stories from your trip to London. You need some stability in your life, and he doesn't seem able to provide that."

"You're wrong, Blanche." I could count on one hand the number of times I had said those words to my sister. They leaped forth right then and there, and others followed with just as much vigor and conviction. "I'm the strongest I've been in years! For the first time in a long while, I'm not obsessing over food or Paul or the fact that I can't find a decent job. Don't you see that everything that happened in London—no matter how crazy and unbelievable—helped me break free?"

"What's next, then?" she asked with the oh-so-familiar sigh of impatience.

"Well, I was thinking I could stay here for a while… since you're leaving and all." I chewed on my lip after revealing the little plan I had come up with while trying to make my way through a sleepless night.

"You don't want to go back to your place, do you?" she asked, as more of an affirmation than a question.

"Just to pack up a few things. That's it. It's calm and… and neutral here. Without the memories. You can't tell me it's mentally healthy to stay in that place after everything that's happened over the years. I tried to end it all, Blanche! Right there in that bathroom! But Paul wouldn't consider moving even when I told him I got shaky every time I set foot on that tile floor."

"You never told me." Her usually firm voice softened.

"I thought it was my fault."

"Nothing is your fault," she said, taking me in her arms and stroking my hair. "I'm sorry if I didn't understand you, Kat. I simply wanted the best for you."

I could tell she was sniffling back a few tears. I pretended not to notice. For some reason, I never liked seeing signs of weakness in my sister. She was encroaching on my territory. I had to see Blanche as the strong one.

"Everything's OK, Blanche," I whispered.

She took a step back, wiped her eyes and smiled.

"You might want to move into my bedroom after I leave. It's more comfortable."

May 1, later

I got off the subway at Columbus Circle, made my way through the mayhem of taxis, shopping bags and traffic lights, and wandered into Central Park. I took in a few great gulps of air as I walked through the grass and then stopped in front of the only somewhat available bench in sight. A man was diligently polishing a small copper square. In memory of the lovely Jean. The words appeared brilliantly under the soiled cloth.

He turned around suddenly and blushed.

"Sorry, I was finishing up here." His hands trembled as he gathered up a leather briefcase and a well-read copy of *The New York Times*. "You probably want to have a seat."

"She must have been pretty special," I said.

"Yes, she was." He smiled and then took a step back.

"I don't have to sit down, actually. Please stay. Continue…"

"No, no," he said. "I have to be on my way. Work to be done. It's your turn to enjoy Jean's bench."

"Thank you." But he didn't hear my words. His well-shined shoes were already traveling along the dusty path, leaving me alone on the cleanest seat in the park. I don't know how long I remained there, contemplating a bird's nest in a tree facing me, but somehow, by the time I was ready to leave, I was also ready to visit the address printed on the crumpled paper in my hand. I followed what remained of the man's footsteps and then turned northwest toward Broadway.

❧

The gallery was nestled between an upscale card shop and an antique dealer specializing in the era of Louis XIV. My observations from afar. The breeze tickling my bare legs, I stood on the center island and gazed through the glass at the black and white prints that looked blurry in the distance. Then back to the card shop with its dainty pink lace envelopes in the window. Then a glance at the dark chest wobbling out the antique shop door ahead of a young man, who was pushing it with all of his might. An older man with an impatient air hurried ahead and seemed to drag him around the corner with just the look of an eye. A group of giggling girls emerged from the card shop followed by the sound of wind chimes.

I took a slow, deep breath and exhaled. I didn't come here to watch the comings and goings in the neighborhood. I came to see Will's gallery. A brave voice from within had been arguing with my own sense of reason. It urged me to march right into the shop, ask for Will and throw myself into his arms. I rolled my eyes at the mere thought. In reality, I could hardly take one step forward.

I squinted. Will wasn't there. I was convinced of it. The gallery wasn't any bigger than the little stationery place next door, so I would have seen him by this point. Bravery, or most likely curiosity, was gaining force. I inched ahead.

And then, before I could change my mind, I was standing in front of the window and admiring photos of Australian and African wildlife. It seemed that his specialty was wild cats. A photo of lion cubs rolling around in the brush held my attention for a long while, and then a feeling of panic seized me. What was I planning on doing if Will showed up? He could walk around the corner at any moment.

My eyes scanned the shop one last time. The panthers, cheetahs, deserts, greenery and burnt-out land. The young woman with dangling pearl earrings who was immersed in a phone conversation behind the register. The narrow wooden door that led to a back room filled with maybe even more of

Will's photos. I swallowed hard and turned around. I couldn't stay here any longer. If I did, I would probably make a mistake. Tears streamed down my cheeks. I started to run. And I ran for several blocks down Broadway's winding path, dodging old couples wheeling home their groceries, school kids playing hopscotch, and a few homeless men who asked if I had spare change.

May 2, middle of the night

This is what I could remember: running, running, running through the early morning streets, damp, wet and grim. The click-clacking sound of my shoes tapping raggedly against the ground. I couldn't breathe. That man's face again. Did I know him? He was running at my side. He was telling me to slow down. The carriage was straight ahead. But I was shaking my head and pushing him away. Then he gripped my shoulders and wrenched me to a stop.

"Don't you see that revenge is the only way?" His clipped words echoed in my ears. "You know what we must do, don't you?"

"I do not want to!" I was yelling now. "No matter what, I refuse!"

"Do you want to be betrayed for the rest of your life? Do you wish to allow such unseemly goings-on? You, of all people, with your pride? Come now…"

I collapsed into his arms. And then all went black.

The nightmares wouldn't release me from their grip. They were chapters in a story that was unfolding. But why? Why this nonsense? If I wanted a good story, I would go to the bookstore.

I rubbed my eyes and read my description of the episode over and over. Then I compared it with what I had written several days ago. I didn't want any part of these people and their tragic story. The feelings of sadness and loss choked me with each and every image.

I thought of Destiny and her outrageous display, which seemed to truly unleash this cascade of nightmares. This was probably part of my own overactive imagination, stimulated by the tale of Victoria and Jonathan. I was being ridiculous for remembering every detail of her monologue and for doubting my own sense of reason. I kept telling myself that my worries about the dreams were silly. After all, with Destiny's words drifting around in my head, how could I possibly have a peaceful night?

May 2, continued

My mother called. Blanche had told her everything, and she wanted to see me. She would be expecting me on the 10:05 train the next day. That way, she could pick me up from the station on her way back from the perfectly scheduled biweekly trip to the greengrocer.

"I think you should spend the night at the house," she said, her voice firm.

"Damn it, Blanche..." I mumbled the words over and over.

"What was that?"

"Nothing."

"Well, don't sound so excited about coming home! I never see you any more, Kat! You hardly ever return my calls, and when I do get you on the line, you're in a rush."

I could see her sitting in front of the soap opera that she wasn't really watching and winding the phone cord anxiously around her fingers. Preferring the dimness of the browns and beiges of the living room to the sunshine beyond. The house was claustrophobic. There were too many memories of tears, nightmares and loneliness. She had to feel it too, yet she basked in this type of environment.

"If you want to see me, Mom, why don't you take a train into the city?" I said, throwing the bait that I knew would be refused. "I'll meet you at Grand Central."

"No, no, you know how I hate the city. Who needs that

dirty mess anyway? Ever since you've been there, you've had nothing but trouble. You should be happy to spend some time at home, Kat. I don't understand you!"

I rolled my eyes. I could feel the familiar knot forming in my stomach.

"Sharon Goldstein next door—her daughter comes home every weekend. They go out shopping together. Or lunch. I couldn't even hope for that with you. I guess I have to accept it."

"Yeah, I guess you do," I said.

"What's that supposed to mean?"

"Look Mom, I don't have time for this..."

"What else do you have to do, Katherine? You're not working."

"Well, I have to look for work, and that takes time too!"

The conversation was going nowhere. As usual. I could have strangled Blanche right then and there. Why did she have to open her big mouth and tell Mom about London and my breakup with Paul? I'm sure her excuse was that since she was about to leave, she wanted to make sure someone else knew what I had gone through and was prepared to look out for me. Another suicide watch.

"Mom, I thought you'd want to see Blanche before she takes off for another part of the world."

"I saw Blanche last weekend, when she came to say good-bye."

My mother sighed on the other end of the line. Then, a few seconds later, she was cooing after her poodle Mimi. That was a good sign, meaning her interest in me was waning.

"Please make sure you get to the station on time to catch the right train—not like last time! I'm not driving all the way up to New Haven because you got on the express. I'll see you tomorrow, Katherine."

"Yeah... tomorrow."

I sank into the couch and scowled. I felt like calling Blanche immediately and giving her a piece of my mind, but I couldn't do that to her on her last day of work before the move. It wasn't as if she'd told Mom everything because she wanted me to be miserable. But sometimes I wondered how

Blanche—who seemed so practical and sharp—could accept the dysfunctional nature of our relationship with our mother. She didn't seem to mind making the efforts to see Mom. And the constant criticism of our clothes, hairstyles and ways of life didn't bother my sister either.

"I listen to her with one ear, and then I go home and do whatever I want," Blanche had told me once. "I would rather go see her—that way, at least she doesn't have the opportunity to criticize my apartment!"

I could understand Blanche's point, but in the heat of an intense conversation with my mother, I had trouble remembering such logical, calm ideas. Even after a few months of keeping my journal, it was only at this point that I could transfer my feelings about her to paper.

May 3

I skipped out on her. I made it to Stamford and even set foot on the platform. But when I saw the white Audi, engine already rumbling nervously, I took a step back. Mom was craning her neck to pluck me out of the crowd.

I couldn't do it. I couldn't take one more bad mood. One more criticism. One more "Give Mimi a kiss like a nice girl." Not now. I slipped back inside. The door rolled shut behind me. I turned off my cell phone. At the next stop, I got out and waited for the next train back to the city. I was home in time to meet Blanche for lunch at the deli.

ೕೕ

"What are you doing here?" she asked, startled. She pushed her copy of *Vogue* out of the way and leaned forward as I settled down in the noisy little corner. Blanche came here almost every Saturday for a soup and sandwich combo. We caught the waiter's eye, and Blanche held up two fingers. He was used to the routine: Blanche would order, and then I would arrive late and double the request even though I would only nibble my way through a quarter of it.

"You were supposed to be going home for the day."

"Yeah, right," I said, rolling my eyes. "I must have been a moron to take that train. I mean, this is your last day here! I'm seeing you off at the airport tomorrow."

I tried to swallow the lump forming in my throat, but it wouldn't go away.

"I'll be back soon," Blanche said. She took my hand. "Every couple of months, I'll be back for a week, Kat. The time will fly."

As usual, she was the strong and solid one.

"You're right. I don't want to make you feel bad."

"I thought you would be angry with me for telling Mom about your London stories. I didn't tell her everything, you know—just enough so she would realize you're a bit fragile at the moment and she should take it easy on you."

I snorted. "Well that didn't work. Our conversation yesterday was more of the usual."

"I'm sorry. I only wanted to do the right thing. I said you broke up with Paul and you met someone in London. And I told her that, perhaps, you would see him here in New York... but things were kind of difficult for you."

"Don't worry about it."

The waiter arrived with two steaming bowls of chicken broth and hot pastrami sliding out from thin slices of rye.

"Why do you always copy my order?" Blanche asked. "You never eat the pastrami. You only munch on the corners of the bread. Why not try something you might actually like?"

"I guess it's a habit... following you."

"You don't follow or listen to me all of the time—at least not lately," she said, taking a bite of her sandwich.

"Let's say I'm trying to break away." And I meant it.

May 4

Blanche was gone. Up, up and away. I felt like a child waving goodbye to her at the airport. Watching her disappear behind the security check. She was off to London for three days and then would be heading to Japan. I refused to cry. I beamed with fake joy, as if I were on Broadway aiming for a Tony.

I had my meltdown as I sank into the taxi's grimy backseat and asked the driver to take me to Central Park so I could spend some time on Jean's bench before the sun set.

Then I pushed thoughts of my sister into the back of my mind. I refused to dwell on the nasty messages my mother had left on my cell phone. I had to concentrate on the future.

It was peaceful here. The birds were busy, twittering about in the nest that I could see so clearly from this vantage point. A few joggers bounced by, followed by a couple of women pushing pink and yellow strollers. I tried to picture Jean, a beautiful and free-spirited young woman running through the grass, stopping to sniff a few daisies. For a moment, her face melded with that of Destiny. I wanted to be like this stranger known to me only through my imagination.

My thoughts wandered back to my own predicament. The question was simple: Did I truly want to see Will?

I knew where I could find him. He was a few blocks away. In a matter of minutes, we could be reunited. What was I waiting for anyway? Jean would have surely jumped at such an occasion.

I sighed and looked down, studying the crumbs left behind from someone's pastrami on rye. A wren hopped over, pecked at them and proudly carried off the biggest one. Why couldn't I be so self-assured and decisive? I shook my head, feeling silly with my comparison. The questions before me might have been straightforward, but the answers were much more difficult. And no, I wasn't making excuses. Of course I wanted to be with Will. But there was one major problem. I had the feeling Will would lead me through more doors that I didn't want to open.

May 12

I couldn't stop shaking. The newspaper quivered recklessly in my hands for God-only-knew-how-long until finally those dreaded words came into focus once again. She was gone. Forever. The news delivered through an ad in the personals. Sandwiched between the men-seeking-women and help wanted listings. Right near the ads looking for editorial staff. So I couldn't possibly miss it.

My heart pounded through my ears as I read the words over and over. Words from Will, who had combed the streets of New York to find me. Words that brought only a painful truth.

> **Looking for Katherine of London hotel art fame and stories of a past together. Destiny has left us. Come to the gallery. May 12, 13 until midnight. I have to find you, to tell you everything.**

Tears drowned my eyes as I threw the paper aside and held my head in my hands. A profound sense of loss. I cursed myself for turning my back on her, for running away, for being childish. Did I actually think she would make it through? My naïve mind really thought that Destiny was above the ravages of terminal illness? I spent an hour or two curled into the fetal position on Blanche's bed. I squeezed an oversized pillow against my damp cheek.

Who was Destiny, after all? I asked myself. And why hadn't I tried to find out more when she was alive? Granted, she was pretty evasive, but my attempts were feeble at best. When I dried my eyes, I knew what I had to do. Numbly, I slipped onto the desk chair, and with a few clicks of the mouse, found a short article about Destiny's demise.

Two paragraphs in a British tabloid summed up the life of a young woman who made rare but memorable appearances at a swanky hotel, ran a teahouse for the fun of it and touted her abilities as the best medium in London. Medium to the rich and famous, who secretly sought her out. My mouth went dry. The stories flooded my head, the scent of champagne filled my nose. The parties. Sam's words. Illusion. Then Destiny's voice rang in my ears over and over again.

"So Katherine, now do you believe?"

୬∘ન્ટ

That was the last thing I could remember when I came to around 7 p.m. I took a few deep breaths, splashed water on my face and looked emptily into the somber eyes reflected in the mirror. I turned away in disgust and returned to Blanche's bed with my journal. After writing about the whole episode, I would have expected to feel some sense of calm, of acceptance. Yet, I didn't. The loss widened and deepened within my heart.

I hardly knew Destiny, yet letting go of this near stranger seemed almost impossible. How could she leave everything unresolved? No, what I was thinking was ridiculous. She didn't choose to die. I was being selfish. She had tried to deliver a message to me—whether it was true or not was another story—and I had refused to accept it.

There, I admitted it. Right there in ink on paper. She had done her best, and I turned my back on her.

I glanced at the clock again. Nine o'clock. Three more hours. Would he really be there, waiting for me?

May 12, late, very late

I ran out the door and through the streets like a maniac, took the subway to Columbus Circle and then kept running. Blind to the passersby. Blind to the city lights, the laughter, the fighting. I knew this route by heart, having traveled it several times in my imagination since my single visit to the gallery.

And then I was there. Standing in the center island, looking across the street and into the one ground-floor window that twinkled with light. He was there. Alone. Leaning against the counter and writing fast and furiously. Mechanically, I lowered myself onto the cold iron bench and studied his every move. What was he writing? What was he thinking as he looked intently at his work? I remained in this trancelike state until he threw down his pen and hurried to the window.

In a panic, I sank back, half hidden by the shrubbery. He glanced around and returned to the counter. I looked at my watch as it struck midnight. How much longer would he wait? Five minutes passed. He continued to write. Ten minutes.

Then, in what seemed like a single instant, he slammed his notebook shut, hurried to the door, dimmed the lights and turned his key in the lock. I wanted to run to him as he stood there, looking left and right and shaking his head. But I didn't move. Something held me frozen to the spot. Frozen until he had rounded the corner and disappeared from sight.

My eyes settled on my watch once again. 12:30 a.m. I had

come all this way to sit on a bench and study Will from afar. I was an idiot. Who was I kidding? An imaginary force wasn't holding me back. I was holding myself back, sheltering myself from the truth, from Will, from everything that terrified me. As I had always done.

I wanted to kick myself out of frustration, yet at the same time, I felt a perverse twinge of pride regarding my self-control. Finally, I was in charge. At the moment, that sensation outweighed any other.

An hour later, I pulled the comforter up to my chin and gazed at the moonlight that sent a dewy beam across the pages I had been filling for months with my sloppy, lopsided writing. Destiny and her stories had wreaked havoc on my life. But for some strange reason, the craziness she brought had nearly washed away my illness. As if there wasn't room for it any more. Was it too early to cry out the word recovery? Maybe. Maybe not. I didn't want to jinx myself.

May 13, early in the morning

For the first time since Blanche left, I answered the phone. Mom. I knew it would be her. The messages had been piling up, and I hadn't returned a single call. I guess I could have let the game continue. It's not as if she would show up on the doorstep. Even if I dropped dead, she wouldn't move her ass out of Stamford. But I was getting tired of that damn ringing and the same old message over and over.

"Katherine, what's gotten into you?"

Nice opener. I pushed away my pile of pillows and propped myself up on one elbow.

"Well?" she said.

"There's nothing like saying hello first."

"I'm not in the mood for sarcasm, young lady."

I snorted and shook my head. Yes, I was still 15 years old sometimes.

"Why didn't you show up at the station? And why haven't you returned my calls? What's going on with you?"

"Nothing, Mom! I felt it was more important to spend time with Blanche on her last weekend in New York."

"And you couldn't have told me that? So I didn't have to sit there wondering where you were?"

"You wouldn't understand."

"Don't treat me like a fool, Katherine."

"How exactly am I supposed to treat you? When you refuse to take a step forward into my life or Blanche's life!

We're always the ones who have to take a step back to who we were a long time ago, to that life we led back there. Everything is different now. Why can't you accept that? There's nothing wrong with change..."

"You're not making any sense!"

"Yes, I am, and you know it!" I sat up and pounded my fist into a pillow. "Ever since Dad left us, your center of attention has been soap operas and your dog. Maybe Blanche has always been too polite to say it, but I'm not. Maybe Blanche is able to swallow it up, and that's why she's always been your favorite."

"You're wrong."

"Oh really? Then prove me wrong. Come here to Blanche's place for a visit. That would prove me wrong."

"You're being ridiculous."

"Think whatever you like."

"Katherine, have you been eating? I'm worried."

"I've been doing perfectly fine, thank you!" I said, between gritted teeth.

"Mimi, come here honey..." Her voice trailed off.

"Listen, Mom, I have things to do."

"That means you're too busy to talk with your own mother?"

"Whenever you want to talk, you know where to find me. Hop on the train."

Before she could say another word, I slammed the phone into its cradle.

I was tired of her, that stupid house in Stamford and everything about suburban life. Maybe Dad had his reasons for leaving us. But I didn't want to think of that. I had pushed him out of my mind for so long that I wasn't about to let him back in now.

May 13, a minute before midnight

I don't remember how I got through the day or how I felt as I hurried north along Broadway. I refused to think of my mother and the conversation that shamed me. I had always been able to contain the frustration and hurt. Why now, today, had I snapped? It was as if my whole life had reached the boiling point.

Everything was a blank until I tapped softly on the windowpane and caught Will's eye through the glass. In an instant, he was opening the door. Tears streamed down my cheeks as I fell into his arms.

"I almost thought you wouldn't come," he whispered, his lips brushing against my hair. My heart beat wildly. Sadness. Elation. Confusion.

I shook my head, but couldn't speak.

"I'm sorry I had to announce the news that way."

"It's not your fault," I mumbled. "But I don't understand. You have more to tell me?"

I took a step back and looked into his eyes.

"Let's go back to my place, where we can talk," he said.

Five minutes later. Around the block, and three stories high. A charming brownstone apartment decorated in various shades of gray and splotches of red here and there. We settled on the couch facing a naked bay window, but I didn't pay a bit of attention to the view. I only could focus on Will.

He handed me a glass of Petrus-Pomerol. The red wine

traced a smooth journey down my throat, and I prayed that it soon would have a calming effect on me.

"Destiny was a medium, Kat."

"I know that. After seeing your message, I found an article on the Internet."

Will grinned.

"I shouldn't have doubted your investigative skills."

"That's why you called me here? To tell me that she was a medium, so I should believe everything she said."

"That's only part of it," he said.

"I'm listening."

He hesitated, took a sip of wine and set his glass down on the translucent coffee table. I had finished mine and was already feeling woozy.

"I also have... a sixth sense."

I furrowed my brow.

"Isn't that a bit of a coincidence?" I asked, my usual skepticism prevailing.

"Not really, considering how we met. A few years ago, I realized I had these... abilities. I was living in London and had heard about Destiny. So I went to see her. She's the one who helped me develop my senses, and she's also the one who uncovered the story. The story about us."

"You expect me to believe both of you? Just like that."

"I don't expect anything. There are things I hope for though."

They say the eyes are the window to the soul. And at that moment, they drew me in, deeper than I would have dared to go. Will's sincerity, pain and desire wouldn't release me.

He was leaning closer, and in what seemed like a split second, our lips touched. Each movement simultaneous, perfect. His skin against mine felt like a new discovery, and then all at once, familiar.

At that moment, I didn't care what was or wasn't true. I could only focus on everything that my senses could absorb. The softness of his cotton shirt as I unbuttoned it, the fresh woodsy scent of his skin, the sound of my laughter as I fumbled with my own buttons, the feeling of my heart pounding as our bodies moved together and the taste of delirium as we remained entangled in that long-awaited bliss.

৩৯৬

A dull ache. My head was throbbing. Where was I? I was curled up, alone in a strange bed. Large, flat green leaves half shaded the window facing me. I sat up with a start. Will. Memories of the night before flooded my mind. I couldn't help laughing giddily, then stopped.

What had I been thinking? I had come to talk with Will, to clarify the situation. And instead, I ended up sleeping with him and feeling so dazed that I could hardly remember anything of our conversation. Except the part about him being... well, kind of like Destiny. I pushed the silky white sheet aside and a piece of paper fluttered into my hand.

Dear Kat,

You looked so peaceful this morning that I didn't dare wake you. I'm sorry I had to dash off to an early appointment. Last night was wonderful. Please meet me for lunch today. How about the coffee shop across from my gallery around 1?
Will

I needed to take a step back. I had let things run out of control, and I knew that if I met Will in the next couple of hours, history would repeat itself. I have to get out of here, I thought to myself. Before my heart overruled my mind.

May 14, late

I couldn't stop coughing. The cloud of dust choked me as I ran up the narrow wooden spiral staircase into a room that I had never before dared to enter. I jiggled the latch until it sprung open and nearly fell into the attic. It was a jumbled little space filled with traveling trunks, stacks of correspondence and a few old chairs that hadn't found their place in the living rooms. Here, the dust was thicker. It mixed with the tears that spilled from my eyes. I advanced clumsily, tripping over the heavy skirt that fell to the ground in thick, voluptuous folds.

I clenched the silky material, finding my pocket, feeling for the hard, pointed object I had stolen from the kitchen. My heart had been pounding double time as I searched recklessly in the place that wasn't my domain.

At once, the sound of voices downstairs startled me. I could no longer hesitate. It was over. The pain, my mistakes. I had to set him free. He would suffer at first, but he would be better off without me in the end.

Knife slitting through fragile skin. Heart pounding, knees shaking.

Darkness. Silence. What seemed like a second turned into eternity.

Blinding light. Voices.

Jonathan's voice.

"No! No, no, no!" I could hear his anguish.

Madness. Silence.

ھوجھ

That was it. The finale to the nightmares that had been haunting me these past several weeks. My hands shook as I wrote the details in my journal. The details that matched Destiny's story. I had seen it through my very own eyes and felt it within my very own heart.

Some would have said Destiny had such a power over me that she had provoked a series of outlandish nightmares. Maybe I would have said this myself a month or two ago. But what I had experienced wasn't simply a dream. It was a memory of the past. There, I had admitted it. Admitted what I had been afraid to affirm for so long. Accepted what seemed unacceptable, illogical.

Well, maybe life was more than logic and scientific explanations. I thought of Will and how I had felt when I first saw him—the déjà vu, the dreams. Then there was Destiny's analysis of my suicidal tendencies. A carryover from a past life? It sounded preposterous at first, but it was beginning to make a bit of sense.

A feeling of elation washed over me. Finally, a reason. A real reason for my pain. I wasn't crazy. I had *never* been crazy. My sadness had always been for a good reason, buried deep inside. So hidden, that even I couldn't find it.

All Destiny had said was true.

May 15

Dear Will,

I'm sorry I ran out on you and haven't answered your calls. I don't regret what happened between us even though to you it might seem that way. For weeks, I longed for that moment, for the chance to touch you, to look into your eyes, to grasp the desires that had haunted me for weeks and weeks... And then it happened, and it was perfect.

You're probably wondering why I've run away. It's because I realized all Destiny said was true. Yes, I've finally accepted it. No matter how impossible and fantastic the story may seem, I believe it. Destiny's death was probably the catalyst, shaking up everything that had been firmly set in my mind.

There have been too many coincidences, too many dreams, too many feelings leading me down the same road. I still don't understand how Destiny knew all that she did—about me, then and now. About you. About everyone, it seems. OK, she was a medium, but what does that really mean? That she had access to the deepest secrets of everyone on the planet? Maybe it doesn't matter, anyway. If I'm willing to accept such an outlandish story, I guess I should be willing to accept the mysterious nature of Destiny.

That said, I can't continue this way. I don't want to gather up remnants of the past and try to piece them together. It's too late to continue our story. I have to move forward and can't look back. It's too painful. It's an open wound that can only heal if we forget about each other once and for all. There, I've said it. Please accept my decision, Will. It's the best thing for both of us. We can't live in the past.
Kat

That was the letter I stuffed into Will's mailbox as tears blinded what I considered to be my last view of his gallery. I promised myself I wouldn't return.

May 15, later

The telephone rang at 6:30 p.m. on the dot. My eyes stared at the bulky black antique. Paralyzed. Mesmerized by that old-fashioned "drrringgg" searing itself into my ears. Afraid that Will would be on the line. Irresistible. I had to resist. Finally, silence. I waited exactly one minute, counting the seconds on my watch, and hurried to the portable phone with the light flashing on its back. My heart raced as I pressed the button and listened.

But Will's voice wasn't the one rapidly chattering away. It was Liz. She had to talk with me immediately about the idea I had mentioned to her. "Please call me back as soon as you get this message, Kat. I'm in my office."

She had changed her mind about my article. That was obvious. It was the only scenario that could account for the urgency I had detected in her voice. I hit a combination of buttons on the phone to ring her number right back and settled into the corner of the loveseat. I didn't know what I would say to her. But I did know that I had to do this before I entirely lost my courage.

"Kat! Ah, I'm glad you received the message so quickly. How are things?"

"Fine. And yourself?"

"The usual, deadlines, long hours…" Then she lowered her voice a notch, and I could imagine her sitting there, knitting her eyebrows as she did when she concocted a new story idea.

"Kat, the reason I called is I think it's time to do that story. The one about the London hotel."

"Oh?" I feigned surprise.

"Yes, now listen, I heard about the death of this woman named Destiny—that unusual name stuck in my mind from our conversation. Is she the woman you were speaking of? There can't be many of them."

"Well, yes… I mean, yes, that's her, and I'm sure there aren't a lot of others."

"Perfect. That's what I wanted to hear."

"It's not like I knew her very well or anything." My heart was pounding. I wouldn't even consider writing a big exposé about my short relationship with Destiny. I hoped to focus on the mysterious nature of the hotel, but when I gave it more thought, I realized that the two were irrevocably entwined.

"Doesn't matter. The important thing is an angle involving her presence, the mystery surrounding the hotel and a section on what is happening today. I've made some calls on my own, and no one knows what's going on. The place is up for sale, but nothing is clear. I would like to know if you're still interested in looking into this and writing about it. Or do I offer the story to someone on staff?"

"No, no," I said, the words tumbling out before I could hold them back. "It's my story. I can do it."

"Wonderful. As for the details of payment, deadline… I'll have to call you back tomorrow. I have someone here waiting to see me, and I can't put him off any longer."

The click of the receiver echoed in my ear before I could say another word.

So that was how I ended up ensnared once again in the tangled web Destiny had spun around me many months ago.

May 16

The details were clear and not very surprising. I had free rein to handle the story however I saw fit, as long as Liz received 2,000 words from me by June 1. Less than a month. A quicker turnaround time than usual as Liz was planning to bump another article that wasn't time-sensitive. How could I ever hope to get to the bottom of this complicated story in a few weeks when I couldn't do it in the months leading up to this point? And now, I didn't even have the advantage of Destiny's presence. But I had agreed to it. Too proud, stubborn and possessive to let any other reporter get within a square foot of this story.

It was mine. It had taken over my life since January. Although it had wreaked havoc on my existence in many ways, it also had cured me in a sense. I no longer cared about controlling my eating habits. For the first time in years, the anxiety had disintegrated. Replaced by new reasons for mental turmoil, perhaps.

Still, a nagging feeling wouldn't leave me. Hadn't I uncovered enough strange stories about my past? I was heading forward once again into the territory that only brought unexpected and painful revelations. Returning to the hotel, to memories of Destiny, would bring me closer to everything I had hoped to leave behind. I was putting my recovery in jeopardy. Yet no matter how hard I tried, I couldn't convince myself to pick up the phone and tell Liz to hand the story off to someone else.

༄ঙ্গ

Mom, with her overstuffed carpet bag of a purse under one arm and Mimi under the other, arrived at 1 p.m. and said she had precisely three hours to spend with me. She dropped everything onto the couch and turned to face me. Mimi sniffed a cushion and promptly settled down. She looked like a little white ball of marshmallow fluff.

"Yes, I know you're surprised," Mom said sharply, running a hand through the pageboy that she colored to the cinnamon tint of her youth. "Didn't think I would take you up on your challenge, did you, young lady? Just because you saw me abandoned by your father doesn't mean that I'm defeated by life."

I trembled, seeing the pain in her eyes and hating myself for having contributed to it. Yet, the stubborn bubble of pride that kept me as its prisoner held back the tears and apologies that yearned to surge forth. I took a deep breath, settled down on the couch next to Mimi and asked my mother to have a seat beside me.

"Why did it take you so long?" I whispered.

"To visit you here? In Blanche's apartment, I might add. It would have been nice to see you able to afford your own place."

I sighed in annoyance at her comment, but held back the sarcastic words that would have liked to jump out of my mouth.

"I mean your comments about Dad," I said instead.

"When your husband cheats on you and your daughters watch the situation unfold… It's humiliating, Kat," she murmured. "It gave the two of you a very poor impression of both of us. What bothered me the most was that you girls saw me as a victim. I didn't want to be a victim, Kat, but it seemed to me that no matter what I said or did, you would see me that way."

She was right. I hadn't spoken with my father in years because he was a damn coward who didn't even face up to his transgressions. I remembered how he denied everything until my mother caught him in the act. Yet, instead of putting all of the blame on him, I sometimes had transferred it to Mom. As if through her weakness, she had encouraged his bad behavior.

"I was convinced your anorexia, the suicide attempts—all that was somehow my fault," she continued, her words interrupting my thoughts.

"Mom, that's not true!"

She put her hand on my arm to stop me.

"Listen, I understand that now. Blanche and I have talked about it a lot."

"You have?"

"Don't look so dumbfounded!" she said, shaking her head. "Don't you realize how many conversations we've had about you? Then you wonder why the two of us are close. It's not favoritism in any way, Kat. Our relationship has revolved around you!"

"I didn't know."

"I came here today because the conversation we had gave me quite a jolt. And the fact that you never showed up at the station the other day... What's going on, Kat? I know your relationship with Paul wasn't ideal, but at least it kept you somewhat in check."

"No!" I said, jumping up. "I don't need anyone to babysit me! Paul was cheating on me, Mom! Just like you, I was dumped... Now you know it. That is unless Blanche spilled the beans long ago."

My mother bit her lip and looked down at her rumpled gypsy skirt.

"No, she didn't tell me. I'm sorry that happened to you, Katherine. You should have told me! I could have..."

"Could have what? Mom, you were in this kind of situation yourself. There's nothing anyone can do about it. I didn't want to worry you about the whole thing. It didn't matter anyway."

"You didn't love him?"

"I don't know. That sounds ridiculous, but it's the truth. Oh, in the beginning, I'm sure there was something there, but after a while, things faded. It still hurt though—the betrayal, I mean."

I couldn't believe I was finally having such a frank conversation with my mother. I stopped, seeing a hint of a compassionate smile on her lips. Was she, too, surprised by my candor? I couldn't be sure. But for once, we spent three hours together without one of us ending up hurt or annoyed. We didn't talk about my father, my illness or even Blanche. We went to a hole-in-the-wall café for egg salad sandwiches and coffee, watched the passersby, and for once, tried to be normal. When I told her I was returning to London for an article, I could tell she held back what could have been a deluge of comments. She didn't believe that was the real reason for my trip. And neither did I.

I left New York before I could change my mind. Before Will had time to call, visit or send a note asking why I had pushed him away. Before I had time for regrets, indecision or doubts. I left just in time.

PART II

May 18

A sharp breath caught in my throat as I walked through the door and dropped my suitcase. Exhausted as I was, I bounded forward and seized the familiar silver bag at the foot of the bed. I had completely forgotten about my first purchase of the year. The hat that ended up leaving me uncertain and jittery every time I placed it on my head. I dug deeply into the folds of tissue paper and pulled it out. A piece of paper fluttered to the ground, and I knelt to pick it up.

After reading the words carefully written in perfect cursive, I had to sit down. For a long, long while. I can't remember how much time passed as I sat there reading the following words over and over again:

Dear Katherine,

If you have this note, I'm sure the beautiful hat has found its way back to you. I couldn't believe you left it behind! You should really be more careful when you're packing… I'm sorry, I don't mean to sound like a mother hen, scolding you. But you have to realize the importance of this hat! You must have felt something when you placed it on your head. I know you haven't worn it yet. It scares you, but it shouldn't. You have nothing to be afraid of. This hat is simply part of the story you didn't want to hear. If you wear it for a little while, you'll understand. If I'm still around when you return, I'll explain everything…

Destiny

My hands were shaking. Ever since my first meeting with this woman and her entourage, I had done more than my share of trembling. What was she trying to accomplish? Now I should say what *had she been* trying to accomplish? She was gone, after all. I tried to remind myself of that. She no longer had power over me. But then I swallowed hard and admitted to myself that, even in death, Destiny maintained a hold on my mind—with a vise-like grip. She had asserted her control over it months ago and that control had never waned. I was incapable of breaking free. Yet, would I really be free without her?

I shook my head and tossed the hat back on the bed. I was disgusted and intrigued, excited and bored. My eyes studied the silver bag. Asking who had left this for me would be pointless. I remembered the reaction when I told them about my late night visitor several months ago. They were covering up then, and they would cover up now.

If throwing that hat into the trash would do any good, I wouldn't have hesitated even for a second.

Sure, as usual, Destiny's story sounded absurd. Yet, somehow, all she had told me was true. This, too, might be more than just the delirious ranting of an ill woman. In my heart, I knew that Destiny's mind was nothing but sound right to the very last moment. Once again, everything she had told me would likely prove to be the truth.

So what to do about this hat? This clue of sorts? I forced myself back into the reality of a writer with a deadline. I had to focus on this hotel and the daunting article I had promised to produce in a too-short period of time. Then I would have plenty of opportunities for my own investigations. This excuse comforted me, although I knew it was senseless.

The hat—and the unknown that it represented—made me uneasy. Still, my curiosity pushed me in its direction, begging me to put on that winter hat in the middle of spring. I will do it, I said, trying to bargain with the small, daring part of myself. But not today. Not right away. Decisively, I pushed the hat back into its dark, dusty home and stuffed it into the back of the wardrobe. That didn't mean I would forget about it.

May 19, during the night

"Ah, the tango!" Gabriel exclaimed, raising his glass of champagne and admiring the dancers who glided across the floor. Even surrounded by partygoers gyrating around the bar, he stood out, sparkling like a diamond that had taken human form. The rhythm carried me blindly past Gabriel and through the crowd. I didn't remember how I had made my way to the gathering or understand why I was there.

The lights were so dim. My eyes searched desperately. Looking for Will, Sam, Destiny. Then I remembered Destiny was gone forever, and Will and Sam were both in New York. There, I was thinking straight for once! But that still didn't explain how I had ended up at yet another one of Gabriel's parties. I took a deep breath, scurried past a couple who had almost tangoed right over my bare feet and sat timidly in one of the bucket seats near the window. I tapped my fingers on the lacquered cocktail table and watched the dancers float past. I admired the women's glittery false eyelashes, severe chignons and jewel-toned stiletto heels. I followed their moves, both sharp and graceful, as the music transformed itself from one tango to the next.

Must be the theme for the evening, I said to myself.

"It certainly is," a familiar voice whispered near my ear. "Don't tell me you don't know how to tango!"

I turned with a start, muttering something about how I hadn't realized I had been speaking aloud. Instantly, I recognized the man who had bought me the black hat on the first day of the year. He settled down in the chair next to me and set two glasses of champagne on the table.

"If you don't dance, at least humor me by having a drink!"

"I didn't expect... I mean, what are... What are you doing here?" I asked, stumbling over my words. "I don't even know how I got to this place or..."

"Has anyone ever told you that you ask too many questions?"

He smiled, his strange golden eyes shining, and lifted his glass.

"Come now," he coaxed. "We don't have all night."

Dumbly, I touched my glass to his and took a minute sip. The bubbles swirled around my brain as I studied this man who acted as if meeting me here was the most ordinary thing in the world. He ran a hand over his tanned, bald scalp and flicked a gray silk scarf over his shoulder.

"How do I know you?" I whispered.

"From the hat shop, of course! You haven't forgotten about your gift, have you?"

"No, no, no. Of course not. It was beautiful. Thank you. I... I just... It just seems like... Even then, it was as if you knew me."

I felt the heat rising into my cheeks. I took a great gulp of champagne, followed by another. The bubbles were really going to town.

"I have another gift for you," he said, smiling and taking a brilliant pair of amethyst earrings out of his pocket. Little gold flowers with the stone set in the middle.

Before I could say a word, he had fixed them to my earlobes.

"I can't accept these."

"Don't be ridiculous! Of course you can. Gifts from friends should never be refused. It is impolite, and I shall not approve of it."

"Thank you, then... but really, you didn't have to."

"You should have them," he said.

"What's your name?" I asked, using my boldest voice.

"Zachary Taylor."

"You probably already know mine." I finished the rest of my champagne in one swig.

"Why do you say that?"

I turned to find a fresh glass of champagne where my empty one had been only a few seconds ago.

"Because whenever I'm at one of these parties, the most extraordinary things happen."

He smiled, a kind, paternal expression lighting up his face, but he didn't answer my question. I lifted the second glass to my lips and drained it.

"Come along, Katherine."

He took my hand and led me to the dance floor before I could refuse.

"I don't know how…"

"Not a problem," he said. "I learned this one recently, but when it comes to dance in general, I am an old pro."

Gracelessly, I followed, my feet tripping their way backwards through the complicated steps. A few of the faces seemed familiar. I must have seen them at the other parties. But I felt too woozy to care. My head was spinning from a champagne overdose and the music, which grew louder and louder. The other couples didn't appear to notice my lack of correct attire or my awkward movements. As usual, Gabriel's parties were all about effervescence, pure joy bubbling wildly to the top of an already full glass.

And then, when least expected, it overflowed.

৩৶৹

A piercing scream. I thrashed about in the dark, feeling around for Zachary Taylor's firm hand, which no longer held mine. Where was I? Engulfed in darkness, sweat soaking through my thin cotton nightshirt, my eyelids fighting some invisible force that willed them to remain shut. I bolted upright, knocked over the clock on the night table and managed to flick on a weak light.

Footsteps running down the hall. Voices echoing. In the distance, sirens. I threw a sweatshirt over my head, pulled on the long skirt I had worn the previous day and hurried dizzily out the door.

Still half asleep, reeling between what had unfolded in my dream and what was going on in the hotel, I followed the mazelike hallways. Alone, I rushed to the atrium, beckoned by the sounds of hysterical voices. When I gripped the cold cement wall and looked down, I understood the reason for the commotion. Through a haze of onlookers blocking my view, I glimpsed the form of a woman. She was lying on the marble floor, face down in a pool of blood.

The scream of horror billowing in my throat was silenced by the arrival of an ambulance. My eyes watched every move as it unfolded. The hotel staff, operating in slow motion in time with the police officers' instructions, guests, gripping their robes across their chests and scurrying left and right... And then the paramedics lifted the young woman from the ground. A sequined purple dress hung limply from the lifeless body and traced a streak of blood along the floor. I cringed and felt an icy shiver run down my spine as I got a full view of her black French twist, now half unwound, and her small round face. Not because they were ruined by the impact of her fall, but because I recognized her. She was Audrey, Destiny's best friend.

I pounded the elevator button and got in for a ride to the ground floor. I pushed my way through the crowd, not caring what people said or did. I had to get a closer look. I had to be sure. And then, a second after I took one last glimpse and convinced myself I hadn't been mistaken, I collapsed.

May 19, later

The police officer told me I had been drunk. That's why I wasn't immediately questioned and instead was brought to my room after sliding to unconsciousness next to the outline of Audrey's body.

"I wasn't drinking!" I insisted, my arms folded over my chest. "The screams woke me out of a sound sleep! You saw how disheveled I looked! It's obvious I rolled right out of bed."

"You don't have to explain your drinking habits to me," the young man said. He raised a dubious eye that only succeeded in annoying me further. "As long as you aren't on the road or violent, it's your business."

Casting my gaze to the ground, I hoped to hide the expression of desperation I knew was written all over my face. His observation confirmed that I did indeed spend an evening sharing champagne with Zachary Taylor. A chill ran through my body.

I shouldn't have come back to this place. There were dozens of perfectly good ideas I could have tried to sell to Liz. Instead, I chose to step into this web that would ensnare me once again. The truth of the matter was, I had probably never broken free in the first place. So maybe this wasn't my fault. Maybe I didn't have much choice but to come here and see things—whatever "things" might be—through to the end.

The line of questioning was basic and boring: Did you

know this woman? Had you seen her at any point during your stay at the hotel? How did you learn about her fall? Why did you come downstairs?

My answers: No. No. (I couldn't possibly explain the truth to him.) A scream woke me up. Curiosity like everyone else.

Those were my only comments, and they must have been suitable because after jotting down a few notes, the officer stood up, shook my hand firmly and said the police most likely wouldn't need me for anything else.

৵৹৵

"What is really going on?" my sister asked, leaning across the booth toward me.

Blanche, who was working from the firm's London office for the week, heard from Mom that I was in town. Of course, the woman's death—police wouldn't yet release her name—had already made headlines. Blanche's first thought was to pick up the phone and insist we meet for lunch.

"Why do you always think that whenever something strange happens, I'm involved? This is a murder, Blanche! What could I possibly have to do with that?"

"Ah, so you're certain it's a murder..." Her eyes studied me as I swirled my spoon in a steaming bowl of chicken soup.

"Ask it," I commanded, glaring at her.

"What do you mean?"

"Exactly what you're thinking."

She kept her mask-like expression intact, but underneath it, I could tell she was ready to turn scarlet.

"OK," she said with a sigh. "I was wondering if any of your party friends... well, if they had been partying with this drunk woman."

"And what would that have to do with it?"

"They could end up in some trouble, Kat."

"That's crazy!"

"It's the law."

I pushed my bowl away.

"Why aren't you eating? I hope you're not..."

"No, I'm not having a relapse, if that's what you're

wondering."

"What makes you say it was a murder, Kat?" Blanche whispered. She chewed pensively on a French fry and wouldn't let me escape her gaze.

"Doesn't it seem like a rather odd accident? I don't know if you've ever seen the upper floors overlooking the atrium, but the walls are pretty high. It would be difficult to lose your balance and fall over. And suicide seems highly unlikely. I should know."

"Kat, I didn't mean to bring up something painful."

"No, that's OK," I said. "I'm dealing with things now. Better than ever before—in some cases, that is."

"And in others?"

"Let's not talk about those."

"They're not releasing the name of the victim," Blanche said. "At least not yet."

I swallowed uncomfortably and studied the table.

"I guess that's to be expected," I mumbled. "Questioning hotel guests and then telling nothing."

"They questioned you?"

My cheeks felt hot. I was sure they went from pale to fire engine red in five seconds.

"Yes, but it was nothing."

"They don't question everyone, Katherine."

"Don't call me Katherine with that tone. You know I hate when you do that."

"Why did they question you?"

"I couldn't sleep well, and I heard some noise." I told my story between gulps of chicken broth, hoping the distraction of watching me eat would take her attention away from judging whether or not I was telling the whole truth.

"I threw on some clothes and walked down the hall. I couldn't exactly ignore the commotion. And then when I realized the noise was coming from downstairs, I rushed down to the atrium where the crowd was gathered. They questioned everyone in the area. Only a matter of routine, I guess."

"Did you recognize the woman?"

"That's the same question the police guy asked!"

"Don't be cute."

"No, I don't know her," I lied, rolling my eyes. "Can you please stop playing cops and robbers and let me enjoy my lunch?"

I could tell Blanche wasn't too thrilled about my arrival in London, but she didn't press the issue any further. She studied my every bite, making sure I finished the entire bowl and the piece of bread on the side.

Then she wrinkled her nose and leaned across the table.

"Where's your other earring?"

"What are you talking about?"

"You've got a beautiful amethyst earring that I've never seen before on your right earlobe, but your left one is bare. Don't tell me you lost such a thing..."

My hand flew to my earlobe as my mind wandered back to the conversation with Zachary Taylor that was supposed to have been in a dream. And I was still wearing one of the dream earrings.

May 20, bright and early

I waited outside the agency's front door until a mousy-looking young woman with green glasses unlocked it and guided me to a stiff chair pushed against a bookcase. The entire office—or at least the part I could see—was not much bigger than a walk-in closet. But every wall, shelf and surface was loaded with notebooks, papers and dossiers.

"Neither Mr. or Mrs. Jones have arrived yet," the woman said. "Can I help you with something?"

She looked uncomfortable as she settled down behind an enormous mahogany desk that drowned her thin frame.

"Were they expecting you for a certain account?" she continued.

"I'm here to see about The Grand East Hotel," I said. "I'm... representing a possible buyer."

"Ah!" the woman shuffled through the stacks of papers near the telephone. "I know they've been doing a lot of work on this one. The details should be around here somewhere."

"Who owns the hotel anyway?" I asked. "It seems no one knows."

The sound of a wind chime was followed by hurried steps and a sharp, yet ingratiating voice telling me the information wasn't available to the public. Mr. Jones, who dumped an armload of papers and his briefcase on the communal desk, obviously had arrived.

He introduced himself, shook my hand and then glared at

the young woman.

"Mary Beth, you know this is our most important project at the moment, and I've explicitly told you I shall be the one handling it. If you truly would like to be helpful, post these packages for me please. They have to make it out in this morning's mail."

Mary Beth didn't flinch. She scooped up the thick envelopes, stuffed them into a black canvas bag and made her way to the door. Her eyes remained lowered as she said good-bye to both of us.

"Difficult finding competent help these days," Mr. Jones said, settling down in the chair Mary Beth had vacated. "I know everyone says that, but it's true! Now then, how may I be of assistance?"

"I'm here on behalf of a wealthy New Yorker, who also wishes to remain anonymous."

"What is he or she looking for, exactly?"

"A solid investment. My... client... was interested in learning the history of the hotel. We're aware of the financial details."

"It was erected in the middle of the nineteenth century as a hotel for wealthy businessmen and their families. Very practical since it was—and still is—right near one of the train stations. It burned to the ground several years later and was rebuilt, in keeping with the same style. Throughout the years, it has been extensively refurbished, yet without tarnishing elements such as the grand staircase. The contemporary touches added in recent years make it quite an exquisite and original property."

"Who built the hotel?"

"The family prefers not to provide those sorts of details at the moment."

"Isn't it a matter of public record?"

"Yes and no," Mr. Jones said, trying unsuccessfully to hide his annoyance. "You don't quite understand. This hotel was the project of an investment company that no longer exists. You could say it passed through many hands as time went by."

"But there was always one main owner behind it, isn't that right? That's what people seem to say..."

"People will say anything!" he said, rising swiftly. In an instant, he was holding the door open for me. "Is there anything else I can do to assist you? If so, we shall have to make an appointment. I have several meetings today so I cannot be held up."

May 20, an hour later

I cursed under my breath all the way to Violet's Tea Dream and sat down at a tiny booth in the back corner. It was strange being in this environment once again. I could still see Destiny sitting opposite me, laughing as I fumbled with my book about dream analysis. I didn't actually intend to return. I guess, for me, this teahouse was located in the right place at the right time. I needed to sit down, have a hot drink and think. The whole idea of the hotel's ownership being some kind of secret seemed preposterous.

A minute after I ordered a cup of green tea, I looked up to see Mary Beth timidly opening the door. Her canvas bag was empty, and she craned her neck as if looking for someone. I waved to her and she hurried over to my table.

"Did you follow me here?" I asked. "It seems like too much of a coincidence."

"Yes, that's right," she said, smiling almost mischievously. "Mind if I sit down?"

"Not at all." I kept my voice calm, but my heart was racing. She obviously knew something about The Grand East Hotel and was ready to share the information with me.

"I'm sorry for the way he spoke to you," I said.

"I'm used to it. But he won't be able to continue that behavior with me for much longer. I've got a better offer and am quitting today!"

Her eyes were sparkling.

"That's what you're going to do when you go back to the office?"

"Absolutely. And will they be surprised—probably thinking I didn't have the courage!"

"What made you follow me?"

"Since I'm quitting and don't have much esteem for my current employers, I thought I might be of some help to you regarding the hotel."

She glanced from side to side around the empty tea salon and then leaned closer across the table.

"A wealthy young businessman built the place in the nineteenth century, but it was registered under the name of an investment partnership that he formed with several others. So it's as if this investment company—Liverpool Investors—was actually the original owner. He eventually bought the company out, but continued to use the name Liverpool on all legal documents. The whole thing gets even more complicated when we reach the point of the place burning down. Liverpool was accused of arson. The investors supposedly wanted money from insurance policies."

Mary Beth's eyes were as round as saucers as she pushed unwieldy strands of hair behind her ears, took a breath and continued. I didn't dare say a word, somehow afraid that the slightest interruption might bring her story to an end.

"Nothing was ever proven, as is often the case with that sort of thing. And of course, Liverpool couldn't raise the money to rebuild. At the same time, the owner was going through some kind of personal tragedy. Anyway, to make a long story short, he reorganized under yet another name—Willow Investments—and was somehow able to raise the money he needed through a whole new set of investors. And there you have it! Since then, the controlling stake of the hotel was passed down through generations of the same family. They control everything. But it's not as clear as it seems. Because it was done through a trust fund, which ended up passing through many hands as people married, divorced, died. No one is one hundred percent sure of the exact name of the person running the show today. It could be any one of the eight original families who invested. Many of the children of these families intermarried. They all have stakes in the place, and some are through trust funds as well."

"But you're sure you know the real owner?" I finally asked, bursting with anticipation. "After all of that confusion?"

"Yes," she said solemnly. "Just a few of us who have had access to all of the documents are able to pin it down. Or at least down to the family. And of course, the tax collectors know."

"What's the name? Are you willing to tell me?"

"That's what I came here to do. It's the Taylor family. They've kept their grip on the place in spite of the turmoil throughout the years. You see, the founder's name was Zachary Taylor."

I could feel the color drain from my face. I knew that name very well. But it couldn't be the same! Or could it? Was the Zachary Taylor I knew some great-great grandson? Obviously, he wasn't the original! I shook my head at my own silliness.

"Are you all right?" Mary Beth was asking me.

"Huh?"

"You look like you've seen a ghost."

"No, I'm sorry, I only wanted to say that... I've met a few Taylors around here so was wondering."

"From what I hear, they keep to themselves. They're very, very discreet people. The majority share in the hotel was part of a trust fund for the longest time, and always had been held by one member of the Taylor family."

"Who is that now?"

"That's the one thing I don't know. The Taylor trusts are handled by an attorney who represents the family. And there have been many changes in the past few years. A lot of deaths in the family."

The waitress set my teacup and pot on the table and asked Mary Beth what she would like to order. But Mary Beth jumped to her feet in a flash.

"I can't stay," she said. "I have a job to quit!"

"Why did you tell me this story?" I asked.

"I have nothing to lose, and I had the feeling you might

have something to gain."

And then Mary Beth walked out of my life.

May 20, two hours later

"Um, I'm looking for books about local people who contributed to the city's growth in the mid-nineteenth century," I mumbled over the counter as the librarian simultaneously scanned her computer screen.

"Second floor, take a right and the section is over by the back windows," she said, waving a slim hand in the direction of a large mahogany staircase.

I nearly ran up the steps, blind to the few students and scholarly-looking individuals who lingered here and there. Arriving at the top, it seemed I was the only one on the second floor: this mezzanine, with row after row of shelves bowing under heavy old art and history texts. I hurried to the high-arched windows that let in streaks of daylight.

I found the right section, but locating documents that would be helpful wasn't the easiest task. This I realized after hours spent poring over pages between various moldy bindings. With more and more frustration as time wore on, I slammed each book shut and moved on to the next. Books without photos, others without names of those who were in the photos, and still others with photos only of buildings and downtown streets. And nothing on Liverpool or Willow investment companies or partnerships.

I held my head in my hands and rubbed my aching temples. It was too early to give up, but I felt as if I was running up against a brick wall at every turn.

"How are things coming along?" I looked up with a start to see the same librarian who had directed me to the history section.

"Not too well," I said, leaning gingerly against the wooden chair.

"We have a rather solid collection here," she said. "Are you looking to find references to anyone in particular?"

"I'm looking for photos of someone named Zachary Taylor, who was involved with a group that built The Grand East Hotel." As I blurted out my request, I hoped she wouldn't ask me why I was on such a determined quest for such trivial information.

"We have a few books around the corner that might be helpful…"

She disappeared and returned a minute later with three volumes so antiquated that I wondered if anyone had touched them over the last century. A big puff of dust clouded the air as she set them on the table in front of me.

"These have a lot of old photographs and drawings of society people," she said. "I would think that anyone who had something to do with building up the city at the time would have to turn up here."

And she was right. A half hour later, on page 53 of the second book, my eyes connected with those of Zachary Taylor for the third time.

I took several deep breaths and closed my eyes against those little bright spots that show themselves just before a fainting spell. I counted to 10, then to 20. Finally, I was ready to face the reality that was so upsetting to me. I pressed the yellowed page flat and examined the features that were already familiar. Zachary Taylor, gazing serenely into the camera, had his arm around the waist of a young woman. According to the caption, they had won first place at a charity ball to benefit children in need. I guarded the page with one finger and diligently examined those that followed, but found nothing more. The third volume provided no further clues. With nervous fingers, I turned back to the photo of Zachary Taylor. How could this be? He had a descendent who looked *exactly* like him, as if they were identical twins born a century apart. It was the only logical explanation. But even that seemed unbelievable.

"The library is closing in fifteen minutes, so you'll have to wrap things up." Another librarian's voice broke into my thoughts.

"Can I make a photocopy?" I asked, clutching the book. He nodded and pointed me toward the machine, where I dropped in a couple of coins for a permanent reminder of Zachary Taylor's face.

May 20, late

I was sitting at the hotel's quietest bar trying to drown my confusion in a glass of champagne when Gwen Garnier made her grand entrance. She immediately caught my eye, left the perfect-looking man at her side and rushed over to me.

"Kat! You've returned! You know you missed out on a fabulous exhibit. Tell me, will you work with me on another?"

All of this as she kissed me on both cheeks and sat down in the foamy bucket seat across from me.

"What about your date?" I asked.

She waved her hand in his direction and signaled for him to settle down at a table.

"Oh, he's used to the fact that I'm always running into people," she said with a laugh. "He can wait a few minutes. How about answering my questions?"

I took a sip of champagne and sighed.

"What is it?" Gwen asked, wrinkling her brow.

"Gwen, my life as an artist, if you could call it that, is over. I'm trying to return to what I know. But the problem is even that isn't proving to be very easy."

"What do you mean?"

I gazed at the bubbles that rose endlessly to the surface of my glass.

"I'm writing a magazine article about The Grand East Hotel and everything that's gone on here. But my research is leading me to more questions than answers. I've fallen behind on this thing, and finally I'm wondering if it's one big mistake."

"Why do you say that?"

"I have to get to the bottom of the story about Destiny, those parties, everything. My editor is looking for a piece with a bit of a spark, but what I'm coming up with is a handful of ashes!"

"Don't be so hard on yourself," she said, squeezing my hand. "Things will work out. An article about the hotel is a wonderful idea! I'm sure management would love the publicity!"

I bit my lip. I couldn't tell Gwen about the strange experiences, my meetings with Zachary Taylor and the shocking revelation earlier in the day at the library. What was the point of continuing the conversation? One single part of this story couldn't be isolated from the whole.

"You're right," I lied. "Don't worry about me. I'll be fine. You probably should go back to your poor abandoned date."

Gwen squeezed my hand once again.

"All right, but promise you'll reconsider my offer about working together again."

"We'll see."

"Ah, I know what that means," she said, rolling her eyes. "I won't hold my breath."

I watched her return to the young man whose eyes brightened as she slipped into the chair opposite him. I refused to think about how things could have been with Will. But when my eyes returned to the champagne bubbles, how could I think of anything but the parties that had brought us together?

May 21, during the night

"There's no reason to be afraid of the hat," Zachary Taylor said in his matter-of-fact voice. "You're not five years old, Katherine!"

We were sitting at the same table as the other night at yet another one of Gabriel's parties. At least I assumed it was Gabriel's party because the atmosphere resembled that of the others. He and Sam, however, were nowhere to be found.

My eyes returned to Zachary.

"Why do I get that strange feeling?" I asked, my words heavy, sticking within my throat. Everything—including the formation of sentences—was in slow motion. "When I put on the hat... I feel dizzy, exhausted, frightened."

"You have to make it past that point, Katherine. It's temporary and worth the mental exertion. If you want to understand this whole story, you *have* to put on the hat."

"But for how long?" Many, much more important questions frapped impatiently against the doors of my mind, but I was unable to set them free. I felt as if the words I was pronouncing weren't even formed within my own brain.

Zachary took a sip of champagne and tapped his fingers on the tabletop as if considering a complicated situation. I watched the reflection of his thin fingers as they danced in the opposite direction of the real ones.

"It's not a matter of time, but of feeling," he said. "You will know when you've obtained enough information to better understand the story."

"That's what I wanted to ask… What story? Does this have to do with Destiny?"

"In a way," he said. "But it has more to do with you."

"That doesn't help me much."

He took another sip of champagne and smiled.

"You certainly want me to hold your hand the whole way, don't you?"

"No," I said. "I can do… whatever… on my own! The only thing is I don't understand what… well… what 'whatever' is!"

"Calm down a bit, Katherine," he said, dusting off the lapels of his dustless velvet suit and leaning closer to me.

"I've been running in circles ever since I came here, ever since I met Destiny," I said, finally recovering my true voice. "Now, she's gone, and it hasn't stopped! Not only that, I think it's gotten worse."

Tears of frustration welled up in my eyes, but I refused to let them fall. I pressed my hands against my aching temples. It was as if a French horn was wailing directly into my eardrums.

"Katherine, give this one more chance! You've come too far to abandon the quest. And what about your magazine article?"

"Look, I know this is about Jonathan and Victoria! Destiny told me the whole story, and I accept it even though any normal person would find it completely unbelievable. But that doesn't mean I'm going to live my life by it! There, I've said it! I won't go back to Will, I won't go back to him. I won't, I won't, I won't!"

I jumped up, turned around and ran. Pushing through the crowd of beaded cocktail dresses and floating champagne glasses, I coughed on air that was thick with musky perfume and cigarette smoke. Then I was falling, falling, falling into oblivion.

That was all I could remember after waking up with a start. Yet another piece to the mysterious puzzle that had become my life. Why hadn't I asked Zachary Taylor the important questions? Such as: Why had he contacted me in the first place? What did his life have to do with mine? And most importantly, what did this hat have to do with anything? I could have kicked myself for wasting a precious opportunity.

Then I scolded myself for actually thinking I could ask someone questions in a dream to better understand a real-life situation. Was I finally losing my mind?

ۑۘۑ

"Why are you doing this to us?" Will whispered the words into my ear as he held me against him, our hearts beating rapidly in unison. "Do you know how hard it was for me to track you down?"

"Well you found me," I said, trying to keep my voice cool.

I stepped back and lowered my eyes. I had been on my way out the door when he rounded the corner and took me in his arms.

"Why can't you accept something so good?" Will asked, his hands holding mine.

"Let's go downstairs," I said. "That would be best."

"Rather than discuss this private subject in the privacy of your room?"

"Yes."

Silently, we walked side-by-side to the bar where I had met Gwen. At this middle-of-the-afternoon hour, we were the only customers. Will chose a narrow booth at the back of the room and ordered two glasses of wine that neither of us would end up drinking.

"So you do believe all that Destiny said. That's why I don't understand your decision. Why wouldn't you want to heal the old wounds?"

My eyes searched desperately to escape his gaze, but something kept drawing me into it. I took a deep breath as if the mere gesture could steel me against the lifetime of feelings bubbling up from within.

"They can't be healed, Will. Victoria and Jonathan were different people living in a different world. Even if part of them somehow remains within both of us, so much has changed."

"Such as?"

"Everything! All that we've experienced in the twentieth and twenty-first centuries etc., etc." I couldn't control my sarcasm, but he didn't seem to notice or care.

Then I looked at his hand holding mine across the table. I wouldn't pull away. I would allow myself this gift, this tiny bit of elation.

"Why are you denying yourself happiness?" he asked as if reading my mind.

"Because a relationship would only bring back those painful memories and the nightmares... oh, those terrible nightmares."

"Of Victoria's suicide?"

"Yes," I whispered.

"We could make it through together, Kat. We need each other. You can't give up on us this easily."

"I have to." My voice was hardly a murmur. I could feel the tears burning behind my eyes. "Please, understand me. The past is that and nothing more. And it should stay that way!"

He pushed my hand away in one abrupt gesture.

"What is there to understand?" he asked.

"Will, I care about you, but we're better off apart, leading new, untarnished, healthy lives."

"That's bullshit, and you know it! Say you don't love me, Kat. Go ahead! Try to make it believable."

Tears were running down my cheeks uncontrollably all of a sudden.

"I don't love you!" I said with my Academy Award-winning voice. But what came out as rage was really the pain of saying words that were anything but true.

"Maybe it is better this way, then," Will said, his face drained of most of its color. "At least I can't blame myself for not trying. For the years working with Destiny. For the years of searching two continents for you."

He tossed a few bills onto the table, grabbed his thin corduroy jacket and disappeared through the revolving glass door before I could whisper pathetically under my breath: I lied. I do love you.

May 23

I spent the past day and a half in bed crying, feeling sorry for myself and wondering how I was going to get my life back together. Then, Blanche called and asked if everything was all right. I had forgotten my promise to call her. She was still concerned about me after Audrey's death the other night. I tried not to sound too annoyed or reveal what I was going through mentally as she assailed me with her usual list of questions.

The grand finale of the interrogation: "How are you going to pay for that hotel room?"

My answer: "The magazine is paying. I'm here doing research, remember?"

And that—the panic that set in at the thought of completing a coherent article by my deadline—is what finally propelled me out of bed.

What about your magazine article? Zachary Taylor's words echoed in my head as my eyes caught sight of the hat bag in the back of the closet.

Feeling a chill creep up my neck, I pulled the terrycloth robe tighter around my waist. But this time, I didn't shrink back and slam the door. Gingerly, I reached for the bag, made my way over to the bed, sat down and took a deep breath. I thought back to my dream and then pulled the hat out of the bag.

Even though my argument with Will filled me with

nothing but sadness and regret, at least I had taken charge of the situation. I had made a decision. It didn't matter that it might have been the wrong one. At least I had taken a position.

With this hat, I had to do the same. Either get rid of it, or follow Zachary Taylor's orders. Before I could put any more thought into it, I pushed back a few unruly curls and covered them with the hat.

A slight feeling of dizziness and fatigue as I had felt before. Then anxiety, extreme distress mounting from the pit of my stomach. With the hat still on my head, I sank back into the mound of feather pillows.

ॐ

"I don't think you should go up there!" Zachary said, wildly pulling at my arm. "Think of what you might see. It wouldn't be wise!"

"Leave me alone!" I yelled, taking the wooden stairs two at a time. "What do I care about being wise?" I had heard the screams, but my heart refused to believe it. How could everything have spun so out of control?

The door to the attic was ajar and clouds of dust choked and blinded me as I stumbled over boxes and old travel cases. I could feel her presence, wilted, lost. And then I saw her. Gone forever as blood leaked from her wrists across the wooden floor. My hat fell to the ground as I leaped forward.

"No, no, no!" I screamed over and over as I threw myself over her lifeless body. My hands clung to her long dark hair, and I buried my brow within the folds of her silky skirt. I looked at the solemn face absent of its usual pink glow and pressed my cheek against hers. Silent tears slipped from my face onto hers. I touched her tiny, pale earlobes, wearing the amethyst earrings I had given her merely a week ago.

"Jonathan, get hold of yourself!" Zachary said, pulling at my arm. "It's too late. Don't expose yourself to this."

Then his voice blended into what seemed like dozens of others, and my world went dark.

৵৽

I sat up in a panic, yanked the hat from my head and nearly crushed it against my chest. My whole being was shaking like a leaf. Tears streamed down my cheeks. My throat was so dry I was certain I couldn't utter a word.

Jonathan. It was the hat Jonathan had worn when he discovered Victoria's body. I had seen everything. The amethyst earrings. I touched my ear, which still wore one of them.

I had been in his heart and mind. That was why I felt such sorrow whenever I placed this hat on my head. It was the door to Jonathan's heart. And Zachary Taylor, his best friend, had guided me there.

May 23, a half hour later

As I ran down the street, my sandals splashed through puddles left behind by an early afternoon rainstorm. My heart was beating so hard I felt it would jump out of my chest when my footsteps reached the shopping gallery. I hurried through the doors and pushed past ladies who lunched and mothers with strollers.

The last time I had been to this place had been on the first day of the year. I had never dared to return after the meeting with who I now knew to be Zachary Taylor. The store was the very last one, on an angle of sorts, with its door directly facing the outside world rather than the gallery itself. It was as if in an effort to make use of every inch of London, where space was scarce, someone carved a tunnel between two walls and set up shop.

My footfalls slowed as I reached a brightly colored perfumery followed by a chocolate maker. Floral and sugary scents mixed, turning my stomach. I took a few more steps and looked at the window display of straw hats, yellow cloth cloches, matching gloves and dainty handbags. I had arrived.

A set of three delicate brass bells jingled as I pushed open the door and slipped into the narrow shop. I recognized the same saleswoman who had been working on the first day of the year.

Her red cupid's-bow lips stretched into a smile as she asked if she could help me find something.

"Um, no, thank you. I'm only looking for the moment."

She smiled again and turned back to the scarves she had been folding into perfect squares. Once again, I was the only customer in the store.

I felt uneasy, not quite sure what I was looking for or expecting to find. At random, I made my way over to a display of summer hats. I picked them up, one after the next, examining the details of silk flowers and soft cotton, and studying the labels.

On my fourth hat, I drew in a sharp breath. The brand, printed in small, elegant script, was "Taylor & Hook." With shaking hands, I made my way through the rest and found five others with the same label.

Slowly, I approached the saleswoman and cleared my throat. She looked up with the same serene smile she had worn a few minutes earlier.

"I... um... have one little question now," I said. "I was wondering about the brand 'Taylor & Hook.' Is there anything you can tell me about it? I mean, the origin."

"Always an excellent, elegant hat," she said, slipping around the counter and leading me back to the display. "The label was created in the 1800s by two entrepreneurs, Zachary Taylor and Jonathan Hook."

"He had his hand in everything, didn't he?" The words escaped my mouth.

"Ah, so you have heard of their other business activities!" the woman said, the smile still plastered across her face. "Yes, this is the only fashion-oriented one. It happened by accident from what they say. Mr. Taylor's sister was quite a seamstress and made the most beautiful hats. One day Mr. Hook gave one to his wife as a gift, and she loved it so much, well, her excitement gave Mr. Hook and Mr. Taylor the idea to start selling the hats. They figured if the fashionable Victoria Hook thought the hats were beautiful, so would other women. As it turned out, they were right."

I don't know how I was able to keep my composure as the saleswoman presented me with hats from the latest collection and explained the details of fabrication and design. It was as if the whole scene was unfolding in slow motion.

"Do the families—Taylor and Hook—still own the business?" I finally whispered.

"Oh, no, they sold it about fifty years ago. You know how difficult it is nowadays to have a small family business in this industry. It seems the big fish have swallowed up the little ones! But I assure you the Taylor & Hook creativity and quality remain. May I interest you in trying one on?"

"No, no that's OK," I said, suddenly feeling a bit lightheaded. "I'm in a hurry today. I'll come back another day."

One more bright smile, and the saleswoman returned to her stack of scarves.

$$\wp\!\sim\!\wp$$

What to think of this? The problem was I didn't want to think about it. I didn't want to accept it. It wasn't as if I could even take a step back, pretend that it had nothing to do with me personally, and use this information for my magazine article. And end up locked up once again? No way. I hadn't focused on food, dieting, weight or calories in what seemed like forever. In that sense, I was ready to yell from the rooftops: "It's over! I'm cured!"

But I wasn't cured. I was merely suffering from a different illness. And this was one I couldn't easily identify. What worried me the most was the feeling I was losing my mind. Believing what was unbelievable meant one was going crazy, right? At least that's what I'd always thought. If that was true, I was in serious trouble. In a matter of a few months, I'd had numerous conversations with a man who had lived more than 100 years ago; accepted that I had been part of a romantic tragedy in another century; met the man of my dreams who had also been the man of my dreams in that other life; and had worn a vintage hat to see into the past. And then there were, of course, the mysteries of Destiny's knowledge, Gabriel's parties and so on and so forth…

Damn it! I threw my pen to the floor and then picked it up to continue writing. Seeing the words on paper made me realize how truly insane all of this was—yet any so-called "rational" explanations seemed even more absurd.

And none of this solved the problem of my article. The clock continued ticking.

May 24

"Has any more information been released about the accident?" I asked in a hushed voice as I leaned across the front desk.

Yet another new employee. He looked up at me with a blank, round-eyed stare.

"Excuse me, but I don't know what you're referring to, Ma'am."

"Only a couple of days ago!" I said, exasperated. "The fall?"

A woman with a perfect black chignon gently placed a hand on his arm.

"Nigel, why don't you help this gentleman over here check in, and I'll assist our guest."

Nigel nodded, and with what seemed to be much relief, stepped aside.

"How may I assist you?" the woman asked. "You were asking about the accident, I believe? I recognize you from that night."

I hoped she didn't remember the police had questioned me and kept insisting that I was drunk. My face burned with embarrassment at the thought.

"Yes," I said, trying to push my own feelings out of the way. "I was wondering if they've identified the body or determined what happened."

The woman shook her head. "Nothing so far. I suppose

we should know in the next few days. In any case, we won't find out anything ahead of the public. It will probably be in the tabloids before we learn about it!"

She shook her head again and crossed her arms over the badge that read: Colette, Guest Relations.

"I hope you haven't had any problems. We certainly don't want any disruptions for our guests."

"Everything is fine, thank you."

"It seems like a horrid accident, that's all. But who am I to say?" Then she squinted her eyes and tapped a finger on the counter. "Ah, I think I have an envelope for you... It was left at the desk earlier."

"Oh? I wasn't expecting anything."

My voice might have sounded casual, but my heart skipped a beat as thoughts of Will rushed into my mind.

She handed me a slim, pale-blue envelope with my name and room number written across the top.

"Who left this for me?"

"Unfortunately, I haven't the slightest idea," she said with a shrug. "It came by post in a larger envelope addressed to the hotel. Can I be of help to you with anything else?"

"No thanks, I'm all set," I said over my shoulder as I hurried away and headed toward my room. I ripped the envelope open as I walked, but it was only after sitting down on the bed and taking a deep breath that I unfolded the thin sheet of paper that had been tucked inside.

Dear Katherine,

I have something very important to tell you about Destiny. Meet me at her house tonight at 8 p.m. sharp. I'll feel more comfortable there, almost as if Destiny were with us. Please don't worry and don't be frightened. I'm someone you can trust. I only want to help you in your quest.

Kind regards.

No signature. I read the words over and over as if somehow I would glean important supplementary information that I had earlier neglected to see. Of course, that provided me with little-to-no insight. I chewed on my lip as I gazed at the letter.

What game was this person trying to play? Why couldn't he or she meet me in my room? And was this a close friend or a family member? It didn't seem as if Destiny had anyone in her life besides the group I had met at the parties. Yet this person knew a few things about me.

Maybe I should have had feelings of trepidation about meeting up with a stranger at Destiny's place, but at this point, I wasn't thinking of my personal safety. I had nothing to lose.

May 24, 7:55 p.m.

Hyde Park was abloom with daffodils and wildflowers, and trees boasted their lush green leaves of springtime as the cab chugged through the tail-end of rush-hour traffic and made its way to Kensington Square. A constant shiver had been running up and down my spine since I had received the note summoning me to Destiny's house. That's exactly what it had seemed like: a summons. In the style of Destiny. As if she herself had written it.

The car rolled to a slow and dignified halt, in keeping with the image of the stately homes lining the street. I pressed a wad of bills and a couple of thick, heavy coins into the driver's hand and cringed as I almost walked into the path of an oncoming car. I still hadn't gotten used to the road rules.

Thinking back to my conversations with Destiny, I took each step with a heavy heart. How would it feel to enter that sitting room and know she would never return? I glanced at my watch as I reached the top step. Right on time.

My heart was racing as I rang the bell. Delicate footsteps echoed from within. The latch slipped free, and the door opened.

"Hello Kat." A familiar voice. My breath caught in my throat.

Gwen Garnier took me by the hand and invited me inside.

"What are you doing here?!" I finally managed to say as I followed her into the drawing room. "This doesn't make any sense."

"Don't worry, it will in a moment," she said, smiling and squeezing my hand reassuringly. "Have a seat and make yourself at home—please."

I sat on the velvet chair I had occupied on my previous visit. Gwen had already prepared a pot of tea and handed me a heart-shaped porcelain cup of oolong as she settled down on the loveseat.

"I hope this is all right?" she said.

"It's fine," I said, taking a sip to calm the jitters that were only starting to subside. After all, in spite of the confusing situation, I reminded myself that I normally felt comfortable with Gwen. But what on earth was she doing here? She, who always seemed to be prodding me for information about Destiny…

The drapes were wide open and the French doors ajar to let in a stream of sweet-scented fresh air. The garden was almost overgrown with buds and full blooms of red, yellow, peach, and pink and white roses.

"The scent is wonderful, isn't it?" Gwen said, gazing at the symphony of color before us. "But I must say, a gardener really is needed to take care of them. Destiny did it all herself, but not everyone has such a green thumb!"

She pushed a plate of butter cookies toward me, then took one herself and settled back against the couch. This was the first time I had seen her in jeans, barefoot and without her cell phone.

"Why did you call me here?" I asked, shaking my head in frustration. "And why didn't you tell me you had some kind of relationship with Destiny? At least more of one than I ever did! Why did you keep that from me, Gwen? Why did you act as if you didn't even know her? And the parties? What about that? What kind of charade are you playing anyway?"

She brushed cookie crumbs off her lap and leaned toward me.

"Kat, I'm sorry. I didn't want to lie to you, but I had no choice. I'll explain. Destiny was my cousin. A distant cousin, but a cousin all the same. As adults, we weren't as close as we were as children, but we had a lot of respect for each other.

We helped each other out when we could. That's why I invited you to participate in the art show."

"I still don't get it."

"I was part of the plan to bring you and Will together, Kat."

"What?" I asked, trying in vain to quell my hysteria. "But how did you find me? How did you know I had done the artwork? And what about Dr. Bell?"

"Will saw you one day when you were going into Dr. Bell's office and he *knew*… He had found you. He followed you a couple of times, gathered whatever elements he could and then asked Destiny for help. Destiny knew a lot of my shows involved work done by patients. So I approached Dr. Bell. All of this was meant to be. You have to believe that! Isn't it more than a coincidence that Dr. Bell just so happened to be one of the doctors who recommends his patients express themselves through artwork on the road to recovery? I had worked with him on similar projects in the past. And you have to admit it's pretty amazing your doctor's office is right in Will's neighborhood."

"So you know everything? And you think it's all true even though it seems impossible?"

I was in a state of shock about Gwen's role in this story. I felt as if the matter-of-fact, ambitious Gwen I had met in Dr. Bell's office and worked with a few months ago had disappeared only to be replaced by yet another elusive member of Destiny's world.

"Jonathan and Victoria? You and Will? Of course. I grew up spending summers with Destiny here in London, or she would come to France and stay with us. This ability of hers was there ever since she was a little girl. We accepted it, but it never was easy. So, believe me, I know that for you it must be much more difficult than it was for us as a bunch of kids. When you're a child, it's easier to accept what adults might consider outlandish."

She smiled, as if thinking back to those happy moments with Destiny.

"I learned the Jonathan-Victoria story when Destiny introduced me to Will and asked me to help them out," Gwen continued.

"I need a bit of air," I whispered, rising and walking over to the French doors. She followed and put her hand on my arm.

"Are you OK, Kat? I didn't mean to throw everything at you at once, but I truly thought you should know. I've been feeling guilty and dishonest these past few months. Now that Destiny is gone, I wanted to lay the cards out on the table. At least as far as anything that concerned me. I never wanted to be part of this, but saying 'no' to Destiny was impossible!" Gwen shook her head. "She could be extremely frustrating at times."

"Why were you always asking me questions about Destiny back at the hotel?" I snapped. "Whether I knew her well... And the comments about her interest in art."

"I was hoping you would open up to me about your meetings with her. And I was annoyed she was making those midnight visits rather than dealing with the situation in a less mysterious way. Destiny could never understand how shocking that kind of thing is to the ordinary person. I felt extremely uncomfortable being involved in this whole story, and Destiny had sworn me to secrecy. I knew it must have been horrible for you and that you probably needed a friend. But you held back each time."

I squeezed my eyes shut and thought of the questions that had been clouding my mind for the past few months. Gwen had to have some of the answers.

"OK, if you want to help me, let's get started," I said. "What can you tell me about Gabriel? What about those parties and why does Sam seem to hate Destiny? You've been to the parties, I imagine."

Gwen lowered her eyes and took a deep breath.

"Kat, please sit down."

I followed her back to the loveseat and settled down beside her.

"What's really going on?" I asked, curiosity and frustration overcoming any timidity I felt earlier.

"Kat, as you know, Destiny was a medium. If you believe that, you would believe she could predict certain things, at least those of any importance. Well, Sam really believed. He and Gabriel had been together for three years, and Sam almost instantly had become like a second brother to Destiny. Life was perfect. Until the accident. Gabriel was in a fatal car crash, and Destiny hadn't predicted it. Sam was devastated and hated her for it."

"Wait a minute," I said, my heart racing. "What are you talking about? I met Gabriel!"

"I know."

"Are you trying to tell me that I met a dead person?" But this wasn't completely new. All of a sudden, I thought back to Zachary Taylor. I had met him too. And those other people at the parties. Were they *all* nothing more than a bunch of ghosts? Yet, I had been there. And so had Will, Destiny and Sam. I was 100 percent certain they were all alive, of course. I stated the facts in my mind simply in an effort to make some sense of the situation. My weary brain was now racing in time with my heart. Maybe Destiny had been able to communicate with the dead, but that didn't mean the rest of us could too. Sure, there were my encounters with Zachary Taylor, but I was still convinced they took place in a dreamlike state.

"Look, Kat, don't drive yourself crazy with this," Gwen said, squeezing my hands. "Destiny gave each one of us the opportunity to see what we normally wouldn't see. That's all I can tell you. I actually never went to any of those parties. At first, I wasn't sure they existed. Then, I realized they were larger than life. Sometimes Destiny did get a bit carried away. There was the noise, and the strange happenings. Honestly, I believe the story about Jonathan and Victoria, and that you and Will are carrying parts of them within yourselves. And I believe Destiny was able to communicate with spirits. After that, I don't know what's true and what isn't…"

But I was no longer listening to Gwen with full attention. Bright spots splashed before my eyes and then the room went dark.

May 25, early morning

A stream of sunshine filtered through the drapes and made its way from the foot of the bed to the feather pillow. Squinting through bleary eyes, I wondered where I was and then quickly remembered the previous night. The images clicked through my mind like a 20-second slide show. I sat up with a start and looked down at the outdated floral-print nightshirt that wasn't mine.

The nightshirt, and the entire bedroom for that matter, smelled of lavender. I was in what seemed to be the former maids' quarters, with a slanted ceiling that dropped low over the mahogany dresser against the side wall. I slipped out of bed and stepped onto the glossy wooden floor.

I still felt rather wobbly. How many times had I lost consciousness over the past several months? Fainting had always been my reaction to stress, but now, with every day bringing a new surprise, this was getting to be a habit. True, the problem was nothing compared to the years of battling mentally with my weight and a plate of food, but it almost made me feel worse, out of control.

I had to keep moving forward. I had only been able to conquer my illness so far because of Destiny and the unbelievable events she brought into my life. Would this last? Or would I fall back into the cycle of destruction once I had found the final pieces to Destiny's puzzle?

All of these thoughts ran through my head in one big

jumble as I walked mechanically around the tiny place. My eyes took in the shelves of porcelain figures, the magnificent chest of drawers that seemed much too imposing for such a room and the narrow window overlooking the street.

And then something caught my attention. Just to the right of the window. An old collage of what looked like family photos. I was once again eye-to-eye with Zachary Taylor. Smartly dressed as usual, he gazed proudly into the camera. The photo seemed to be a professional picture from one of the city's best studios. Zachary posed with the same umbrella he had carried with him the day of our first meeting.

I was beyond any state of shock. For once, I maintained my composure. After all, odd stories had been unfolding ever since I met Destiny. I had to ask Gwen about this. And then I wanted to leave this place. This place that brought me much too close to Destiny.

৵৹

Gwen placed a porcelain plate with a warm toasted muffin in front of me along with a cup of freshly cut fruit and a jar of raspberry jam that looked homemade. She poured the tea and then sat down next to me.

"I hope you slept well. If I had thought you would faint, I wouldn't have told you everything, Kat. I didn't want to upset you."

"No, don't worry about it," I said, glancing around the familiar drawing room and taking a sip of Darjeeling. "I've gotten used to it."

"Used to fainting or being upset?"

"Both."

"I know the past few months must have been difficult for you." She shook her head and chewed thoughtfully on a piece of muffin. "Maybe I should have said 'no' to Destiny for once. We shouldn't have brought you here. You were—are—too fragile. I feel as if we took advantage of that. Please don't take this wrong. Most people are too fragile to be bombarded with so much difficult-to-accept information."

"No," I said. "It's best this way. Then it's up to me to

decide what I want to believe and what I want to do with my life."

"You have a point."

I took another sip of tea and glanced back at Gwen. It was now or never.

"Gwen, up in the guest room... the photos on the wall. Are they of the family?"

Gwen nodded.

"Yes, they're family photos, from Destiny's mother's side. The Taylors."

"Ah, I see... and that man in the center of the collage is a great, great uncle or grandfather?"

"He was her great, great, great grandfather. I think that's the right number of 'greats'... A very proud and elegant man. But I don't know much more about that side of the family. The Taylors have always been secretive... Would you care for more tea?"

"No, thank you," I said, hardly hearing those final words.

I was too busy putting two and two together. Destiny was a direct heir of Zachary Taylor. *Destiny's family owned The Grand East Hotel.* That was why no one cared about Gabriel's parties or Destiny's escapades. Of course, Gwen knew more than what she had told me. But I had learned all I possibly could from her about this whole story. She had retreated within and wasn't ready to step out. Sure, she was tired of being part of this plot involving Destiny, Will and me, but there was something more. And she was holding back from me. Something I could never force her to reveal.

Carefully, Gwen stacked our plates and cups onto a little serving tray and dusted a few crumbs off the tea table.

"Can I help you clean up?" I asked.

"No, I wouldn't hear of it!" she said, waving a hand in the air.

"Isn't there anyone around to help out?"

"No," Gwen said with a sigh. "I'm actually here for the next couple of days to neaten the place up and then it's going on the market. Who has the time or energy to take care of such a house? Not one other family member wanted to come to get things ready for the real estate agency. As usual, I got stuck." She shrugged and shook her head.

I glanced around the room one last time, trying to memorize every detail of this souvenir of Destiny. Gwen asked if she could call a taxi, but I told her I would rather walk to the tube station. Sadness and loss suddenly overwhelmed me in much the same way they did on the day I found out about Destiny's death.

More than anything else, I needed fresh air and a walk to clear my head. But even that stroll through the beauty of Kensington Square did little to reassure me. The story of Jonathan and Victoria was difficult enough to swallow. How could I possibly believe that I had met with a man who lived 150 years ago and attended parties with Destiny's deceased brother? At this point, I didn't even care that I now knew the true identity of The Grand East's owners and had what I needed to write my article. When one was going crazy, what would be the importance of such a detail?

May 25, noon

I ran from the tube station and into the pouring rain that wiped away the brightness of the early morning hours. The Grand East Hotel stood tall and gloomy, its gray exterior blending with the darkening sky. Drenched to the skin, I whirled through the revolving doors and hurried to the elevator that swallowed me in one gulp of steel. I hit number four and made my way through the labyrinth to my room. Just one quick stop to throw on dry clothes.

I stripped, tossed my wet top and jeans onto the armchair and pulled on my most comfortable cotton dress and sweater. In less than five minutes, I was ready to go.

But something stopped me. A cream-colored envelope that someone had slipped under the door. It was half rumpled from my damp, rapid footsteps as I had entered the room. I snatched it off the ground and ripped it open.

Four simple words and then a signature:

I don't believe you.
Will

I crushed the paper against my chest and let the tears that had been begging to fall for a million different reasons trickle down my cheeks. I thought back to our argument. He didn't believe what I had said any more than I did. I wasn't that good of an actress. I could never look him straight in the eye, say "I don't love you" and be convincing.

Where was he? Still here in London or had he returned to New York?

I turned the envelope over in my hands and looked inside, but I couldn't find a clue. He most likely had returned home. He couldn't leave his gallery unattended for long.

Wiping away my tears, I stuffed the letter into my suitcase and hurried out the door. Relief washed over me: Will didn't believe the cutting words that had slipped out of my mouth much too easily.

My quest for answers to every question Destiny's presence stirred up was necessary. I wouldn't deny that. But I was still too vulnerable to accept a relationship with Will. And live in the same state of insanity that had overcome me since January? No. I had to uncover the truth about all Destiny had said. That way I could put it behind me forever. Then I had to get on with my life. Alone.

I raced through the dim, empty halls with my feet rather than my eyes guiding the way. Then up, up, up that little ladder at the end of the hall near the highest level, through the trap door and into the room that smelled of fresh paint.

I sat there on cold opaque glass glowing blue beneath me and looked around at the newly completed renovation of this magnificent space that had known so many parties. I could picture the bar to my left and the dance floor in front of me. To the right, near the wide expanse of bay windows, were the tables and chairs where Zachary Taylor and I had shared champagne. I could still feel Will's mouth on mine as I gazed at the window straight ahead. Right there, he had kissed me for the first time.

In my mind, everything was right as it should have been. But when I looked around, there wasn't a single trace of Gabriel's parties. I thought back to my earlier daytime visit to this room while it was under renovation, and I shuddered.

Then I scolded myself for such silliness. What did I really hope to find here? Did I expect to see Gabriel? Or did I wish to meet Zachary Taylor? Something, anything, to prove I wasn't crazy.

And just then, a tiny object on the ground glimmered in the overcast light of a stormy day. I walked across the floor and bent down. The earring. The missing amethyst earring. Exactly where Zachary Taylor and I had been dancing. Numbly, I picked it up and with unsteady hands stabbed it through my earlobe.

This whole story might have seemed impossible, but it wasn't. This was part of the proof. Zachary Taylor was an expert at providing material proof. I wasn't crazy after all. And he, wherever he was, wanted me to know that.

May 26, early morning

I sat at the desk in my hotel room, flipped open my laptop, and for the first time in a year, started writing something other than an entry in my journal. The article about the hotel, Destiny and the mysterious parties spewed forth with such ease it was as if someone else was dictating everything to my fingers as they flew rapidly over the keyboard. I left a few spaces here and there for quotes I had yet to gather.

Then I read my work. I was sure Liz and our readers would be pleased, but to me, the narrative seemed superficial compared with what I had been experiencing since January.

Still, did I have much of a choice? This was supposed to be a factual, yet buoyant, travel article, sparked up with a few sentences about the mysterious laughter trickling down the halls from time to time. Period. It wasn't meant to be an investigative piece, combining tragedy, fantasy and mysticism.

That's your personal story, an internal voice said so quickly I couldn't tell if it was someone else's or simply my own.

I held my head in my hands. Would I make it after leaving The Grand East Hotel, memories of Destiny and all she had brought to my life? Would my attention turn back to that grating anxiety chipping away at my mind? Would the only relief be control over everything that landed on my plate?

I took a deep breath and shook my head as if to rid it of the worries that lingered in dusty corners of my brain. No. I couldn't let it happen. I didn't feel as if it could happen, as a matter of fact. The old worries didn't concern me any more.

Had Destiny been right all along? The anxiety and suicide coming from the wounds of another lifetime? The idea continued to leave me perplexed, but as each day passed, I couldn't help but come one step closer to believing her.

Accepting the story of Jonathan and Victoria had been the catharsis that freed me.

A thump against the door jarred me from my thoughts. The morning paper. I retrieved it and flipped through as I did on most days—not interested in most of the articles, yet afraid of missing something crucial if I didn't at least glance at each page.

The words "Grand East" were the only ones to catch my eye as I scanned to the bottom of the society section. The police had publicly identified Audrey Moss as the woman who died several nights ago at The Grand East Hotel. She was 30 years old and from the Moss family of Kensington. Her death was found to be an accident, according to police. And that was it. A meager paragraph and the story of Audrey Moss was signed, sealed and delivered.

I still didn't think it was as cut-and-dried as that, but I had to admit I didn't have much of a way of proving otherwise. Just because Audrey was Destiny's best friend didn't mean her death was anything more than an accident.

I shook my head and tossed the newspaper aside.

❧

I couldn't help bringing the article about Audrey with me when I met Blanche for lunch a few days before her departure for Japan. We met once again at the hotel's most casual restaurant and chose one of the empty booths in the back. Only after we had ordered two bowls of chicken soup did I broach the subject.

"Did you see this?" I asked, unfolding the newspaper in front of her.

"I thought you didn't want to talk about it," she said coyly while stirring circles in the steaming liquid.

"Well, I changed my mind!"

"You don't have to get testy."

Blanche took a sip and then winced.

"See, that's what happens when it's too hot."

"Katherine, what age are you anyway?" Blanche asked, rolling her eyes at what she likely deemed my immaturity.

"It's not a murder. At least, that's what the police have decided."

"Yes, I saw the article," Blanche said, again rolling her eyes, but this time at the police department's idiocy rather than mine.

"What do you think?" I asked. "It seems weird to me. I mean, it's not like I have any proof, but an accidental death seems impossible. Even if she collapsed, she wouldn't have fallen over that high barrier."

"Well, if you want to know what a lot of my colleagues at the firm think is strange..." She stirred her soup again and sipped it tentatively.

"Go on..."

"Audrey Moss owned a considerable stake in the hotel, and was set to inherit Destiny's share. Destiny willed almost everything to her closest friend. The afternoon preceding the accident, Audrey made a bid for the majority share in the hotel. And her offer was above the asking price."

"Are you serious?" My heart skipped a beat. "How do they know all of that?"

"The other day one of our attorneys lunched with a friend who's working on the case. Of course, the real estate agent was ready to jump on the offer. But when he went back to the attorney acting for the owner, well, the attorney said he wasn't sure if the stake was still for sale. The owner was having doubts. The real estate agent kept pushing to sell, but in the end..."

"What? I don't get it. Didn't they seem hurried to sell and then suddenly it's over?"

"Who knows what goes through people's minds, Kat. The owner has the right to keep his or her share in the hotel or sell it if he or she sees fit. It just seems like quite an odd coincidence that this woman made an offer for the place that day."

"Too odd," I said, forcing myself to swallow several spoonfuls of noodles under my sister's watchful gaze.

"I hope you're not getting any crazy ideas."

"What do you mean?"

"You shouldn't be getting involved in this, Katherine."

"Don't be ridiculous! Why would I even consider it?" I said, half hiding my lying face behind the thick blue napkin.

But she wasn't being ridiculous. She knew me too well.

May 27, early morning

I didn't have much time left. My article was almost complete, which meant my days at The Grand East Hotel were numbered. I would be heading back to New York any time now, but I couldn't leave without *knowing*.

And the only way to find out more was to learn more about Audrey Moss. I had mulled over my possibilities as I tossed and turned through a night when sleep wouldn't come. Will, Sam or one other person. After digging around in my overnight bag, I found what I was looking for: the rumpled business card that Margaret Bloome, Destiny's nurse, had given me.

I remembered her telling me on the day I first visited Destiny's house that several people had come by during the week. It seemed likely one of them would have been Destiny's best friend.

Certain I wouldn't have any luck on the phone, I hopped in a cab and nervously played with the strap of my backpack as the car turned down one dim, narrow street after the next. It was a short ride through the financial district, where imposing buildings loomed overhead, blocking any possible sunlight.

The agency, employing nurses for home healthcare, was situated at the end of an alley next to a block of doctors' and lawyers' offices. I pushed open the glass door and glanced around at the bare, sterile surroundings. A couple of dog-eared posters of smiling nurses holding the hands of grateful patients decorated the walls. Unrealistically, I expected Margaret to pop up out of thin air as if she had been waiting for my arrival.

"May I help you?" A teenager looked across the counter as I approached.

"I'm, uh, looking for Ms. Margaret Bloome, please."

"What's this regarding? A new patient or one of her regulars?"

"It's about a former patient... one who passed away not too long ago. I only need to speak with her for a couple of minutes. I have to ask her something important."

The girl knitted her eyebrows, was about to say something and then bit her lip.

"It's rather basic, really, but urgent," I continued.

"She's in the back," the girl said. "I'll get her for you straight away. If you'd like to have a seat..." She indicated the folding chair in one corner of the vestibule.

"That's OK, I'm all right," I said, leaning against the counter.

My eyes roamed blindly over the piles and piles of paperwork that likely were part of the girl's internship at this office. There wasn't even an inch of bare space on that desk.

Moments later, Margaret Bloome hurried into the room, and I turned around, trying my best to exude a natural sense of confidence.

"I don't know if you remember me," I began.

"You're the young woman I met at Destiny's house," she said, shaking my hand in her efficient manner. "Can I help you with something?"

She clutched a handful of patients' charts in one hand and smoothed the perfect crease in her white pants with the other.

"I'm trying to find the family of Destiny's best friend Audrey Moss. I figured you might be able to help me."

"How so?"

"Well, I thought you must have seen Audrey at some point or heard about her." I felt the heat rising to my face at a much-too-rapid pace.

"You're speaking about the young woman who fell to her death at the hotel. I heard about that, and yes, I've met her."

"I need to get in touch with her family, about something regarding Destiny," I lied. "I know they live in Kensington, but I'm sure there are many of them. I don't know where to start, so I was hoping you might have an idea."

"I don't want any more involvement," Margaret said. "If you ask me, they are—were—all crazy. Those two young women and their friends."

"But you were so protective of Destiny!"

"Of course, she was my patient! That's my job, and I take it very seriously. But I have to say it was difficult staying on to the end. I'm afraid I can't help you with anything further."

"All I need is a name," I said, not caring about the mounting desperation in my voice. "A brother or sister of Audrey... a cousin... someone..."

"Try calling on her sister Charlotte Moss in Notting Hill. She's the only family member I know of by name. There is nothing else I can tell you so there's no point in asking any more questions."

"OK, that's all I need, thank you."

I was about to turn around, but hesitated for a split second.

"Just one little thing," I said. "Why do you think Destiny and Audrey were crazy?"

"They weren't living in reality. Isn't that reason enough?"

&

Phone call to Charlotte Moss. A lilting, childlike voice. Not knowing exactly what to say, I told her I had been a friend of her sister's. My sentence hung strangely in the air as I tried to repeat the well-rehearsed phrases that wouldn't come out of my mouth when I needed them most. But Charlotte didn't seem to notice my discomfort, and before I could say another word, she had invited me to tea.

Charlotte lived on a trendy street packed with antique shops and hangouts for those needing a coffee fix. I stepped out of the double-decker and walked the short distance to her apartment. A brick building squatting atop a hat shop that reminded me of the place where I had first met Zachary

Taylor. I shivered and pushed the thought from my mind. I had to deal with the subject at hand.

A second shiver when Charlotte answered the door.

"I know, I look like Audrey," she said, escorting me through a narrow entrance, up several steps and into a tiny sitting room with flower-printed walls.

"I didn't mean to…" I stumbled for words. Charlotte had her sister's large blue eyes, the same wide smile and shining dark hair. She was a bit rounder and taller, but the differences weren't easy to identify.

"That's all right, I'm used to it. Audrey and I are—were—only a year apart. Some people thought we were twins."

Charlotte sat on the floral-printed sofa and tossed her raspberry-colored shawl onto a cushion. I settled into an armchair facing her and accepted the warm cup she handed to me.

"My question is… How come Audrey never mentioned you to me?"

"I'm sorry," I said, gazing into my own tea reflection. "I exaggerated because I needed to meet someone in her family. Destiny introduced me to Audrey, and then, well, with both of their deaths, I have so many questions and no one has answers."

"Welcome to the club," Charlotte said, her voice revealing a tinge of bitterness.

"I'm sorry… about the accident."

"Thanks… It's difficult." Charlotte blinked away tears, and I looked down, hating to impose on her at such a time.

"I shouldn't have come, but I didn't know where else to turn."

"The problem is it wasn't an accident," Charlotte said, her baby voice suddenly turning adult. With those words, she seemed to steel herself against any sadness.

"What do you mean?"

Her eyes held sparks of anger at whatever circumstances had converged that night at The Grand East Hotel.

"The Taylors killed her," Charlotte hissed almost under her breath.

"What?"

"Look, I'm not saying I have proof of everything, but the story is too suspicious for my taste."

"Why would Destiny's family kill your sister? And who exactly would have done it?"

"Let me start from the beginning," Charlotte said, taking a sip of tea.

My heart was racing as I leaned back against the soft cushion. So I wasn't the only one with doubts...

"Destiny and my sister were both mediums," Charlotte said. "I don't believe in that rubbish and neither does the rest of our family. That's about the only thing we have in common. Audrey was quick to seek refuge with Destiny and her friends. If you're like them, I'm sorry—but I think it's silliness and won't be convinced otherwise."

"Before some recent experiences, I had always been more in your camp than theirs... But things have changed. I can't explain it."

"You don't have to," Charlotte said, smiling and shaking her head. "I'm sure Destiny was the source of those experiences. Anyway, my sister was a regular at Destiny's parties at The Grand East Hotel, and when Destiny passed on, Audrey told me she would continue the parties and whatever else... I told Audrey she was being foolish, but she wouldn't listen! She never listened. At least not to me. I've never been to that particular hotel or to any of those get-togethers, but I do know that someone wanted the commotion to end. That someone is a member of the Taylor family."

I looked up with a start.

"You're surprised I know who has stakes in the hotel?" Charlotte said with a smirk. "Let's just say the Moss and Taylor families are rather close."

"When Audrey threatened to continue the parties, the Taylors weren't too happy about it..." I said.

"Again, I don't have any proof, but that seems like a logical assumption. When Destiny was the one responsible for the craziness, they had to bite the bullet. But after her death... the whole attitude changed. I heard a lot of chatter about the Taylors thinking the hotel might bring them a new investment opportunity. They became determined to clean up the hotel's reputation. My little sister, however, got in the way of that. Destiny left her share of the hotel to Audrey, making my sister the second-biggest owner. Audrey and her big trust fund became the enemy. She had plenty of money like the rest of us, but she took a particular joy in throwing it around. When the Taylors refused her offer for their stake in the place, she told them the parties would continue anyway. They knew she could pull it off. Because she was a lot like Destiny."

I placed my half-empty cup on the end table.

"There is quite a chill in here," Charlotte said, pushing the window shut.

"Audrey told you all of that?"

"She never had a chance to… but I pieced the story together on my own."

"It makes sense. And it's scary. The thing I don't understand is how the whole case was handled. Why was it called an accident after such a short or even nonexistent investigation?"

"Because of the Taylor-Moss connection," she said. "We go way back. Loving each other. Hating each other. Protecting each other."

"This is about protection? But why? That's ridiculous! How could your family protect them if they murdered Audrey? I don't get it…"

"Neither do I and that's why I'm living in this apartment they call tacky rather than at one of our places in Kensington. I have hardly any contact with the rest of them. I was tired of the lies… of the treachery. Who needs it? We're living in modern society, and we have to respect modern rules. But some families are above that. Our families have connections everywhere so they don't obey rules. I couldn't be part of it any longer."

"You're not going to push the subject, then? To look for evidence or find out the name of the one—of the Taylor—who did this…"

"What does it matter?" Charlotte said. "It's a lost cause, Katherine. I'm used to it. I can't fight against them! And what for, anyway? Audrey is gone—it's too late now."

Again, she blinked rapidly against the tears that glistened

in the corners of her eyes, and again, I looked away.

"Tell me, Katherine," she said after a moment. "Do you plan on going any further with this? I hope you don't, because it truly isn't worth it in the end. The best thing to do is to distance yourself from the Taylor and the Moss families. That's what I've done, and it's worked out rather well. For you, it should be much easier. After all, you aren't one of us. That in itself is quite a stroke of good luck."

May 27, night

My hands shook as I held the phone and listened to Will's soft voice on the other end of the line.

"Where are you?" Those had been my first words.

"New York... where you should be too. With me. Did you get my note?"

I could tell he was half smiling, and I couldn't help but do the same.

"Yes, I did."

He could hear my smile through those three little words. We both knew he was winning at this game, but something still forced me to hold out. What was I really trying to accomplish? I had asked myself the question over and over, but had yet to come up with a meaningful answer. Other than the fact that I was scared to truly enter this story, to become a participant. In my mind, I was still a witness, too terrified to cross the line.

"Kat, it's time to make a decision," he said. Again, the gentle, soothing voice. "Destiny is gone... and so is Audrey."

"You did know her..."

"Yes, almost as well as I knew Destiny."

"Do you think she was murdered?"

"I don't know. That's not for us to answer. I'm afraid you're going too far, Kat."

"What do you mean?" A sudden spark of annoyance came to life within me.

"Destiny helped bring us together, Kat. Period. There's no reason to ask yourself questions about her friends, family, parties and way of life. None of that has anything to do with us."

"How can you be so sure?" I snapped.

"She would have told me. And I would have had an idea about it on my own."

"Maybe she didn't know her best friend was going to be murdered. She wasn't even able to predict her own brother's death after all!"

Will drew in a breath. Silence.

"It's not infallible, Kat."

"What isn't?"

"When you're a medium, it doesn't mean that you can forecast the future one hundred percent of the time. There are limitations! Some things are meant to be, and some things aren't."

"Do you mean the information about Gabriel and Audrey was withheld from her? By... well, by whoever?"

"The information wasn't available," he said, correcting me. "There's nothing more to it. Destiny understood the limitations. And I understand them too."

"Sam doesn't?"

"No, he doesn't."

Silence for a moment as I thought back to my original question: Why was it time to make a decision after the deaths of Destiny and Audrey?

"Now that they're gone, there's nothing else for us to learn about our past or future, Kat," he said, as if reading my mind. "It's up to us to move forward. We don't have a crutch of sorts, helping us advance in one direction or another."

"Is that what Destiny was for you?"

"Yes, for me and many others."

"I have this article to finish," I said weakly.

"You're almost done, and that's why you've had time to delve into these new developments."

I had forgotten he had somewhat of a sixth sense too.

"Why is everyone willing to turn their backs on this story?" I said.

"Because the 'everyone' you're referring to understands this is one of those cases that involves powerful people who have control beyond what you could imagine. Their issues have nothing to do with you, and it should stay that way!"

His comments echoed what Charlotte had told me about the two families, but they only enticed me to find out more.

"I need some time, Will," I said, trying to sound detached.

"Kat, time is running out."

"What do you mean?"

"If you wait too long, you'll find out on your own."

Then stiff, uncomfortable good-byes. Both of us seemingly disappointed, regretful.

Another dream, or sort of.

"I see you found the missing earring," Zachary Taylor said with a sly grin as he lifted his champagne glass.

I didn't remember leaving my room or following the labyrinthine path to the party, but there I was: sitting opposite Zachary Taylor at the table we had occupied twice before. He, elegant as ever, wore a dark silk suit. I, as usual, was the only one in the room in a nightgown.

"How did you know I lost it?" I asked. Then I shook my head. "Never mind… silly question."

"Questions are never silly, but I have known a few answers to fall into that category!"

He tasted his champagne and slid another glass across the table to me. A rush of fizz seemed to bubble right up to my brain after the first tentative sip.

"How did I get here?" I asked. "What am I doing here?"

I looked from left to right, but couldn't recognize any familiar faces among the throng of gyrating bodies on the dance floor. A jazzy tune I'd never heard before filled the air. Sequins sparkled on dresses, reflecting the disco balls overhead. A couple, both dressed in silver, swirled apart, and I caught a glimpse of Gabriel sipping champagne at the bar. I jumped to my feet and stepped forward. Like an elastic band, the dancers bounced back into each other's arms and then flew apart once again. The stool Gabriel had occupied a split second ago was empty.

Collapsing into my chair, I turned to Zachary and wrinkled my brow.

"Where's Gabriel?" I whispered. "He was there five seconds ago and then... nothing. He couldn't have disappeared so quickly!"

"My dear Katherine," Zachary said, a knowing look playing across his face. "You're certainly aware of how flighty Gabriel can be. One minute he's here, the next he's there. There's no reason for such distress! Did you want to speak with him for any specific reason?"

"Uh, no. I guess I was relieved to see a familiar face." I rubbed my temples and squeezed my eyes shut. Then I looked up again. Zachary, smiling serenely at me, was still sitting in his chair. "I don't understand why I'm here in the first place! How do I keep arriving at these parties anyway? Nothing makes sense any more..."

"Of course things make sense, Katherine. It depends on how you look at the situation, that's all."

"Well, how should I be looking at this one?"

"You come to these parties seeking information."

"That's not true!" I said, leaning closer to him, then dizzily shifting back into my seat. Too much champagne. That had to be it. My heart was pounding a mile a minute.

"Katherine, a few hours ago, your wish was to find out more about the Taylor and Moss families."

"How did..."

"The mechanics of this aren't important, my dear. What is important is the message I have for you."

"Message?" I asked dumbly.

"Victoria's maiden name was Moss."

I woke with a start and bolted out of bed. Images of disco balls, dancers and Zachary Taylor's smile blinded me as I stumbled over the comforter and flipped on the lights. Trembling in my damp nightgown, I pulled a sweatshirt over my head and burrowed into the armchair. It was a dream, nothing more than a dream. I tried to convince myself of this, but as with all of the other times, I failed.

Zachary Taylor had somehow brought me to him to tell

me that Victoria was a member of the Moss family. The Victoria-Jonathan story gained a new dimension with the passing of each day. But what did this mean? What was I supposed to do with this information?

୨∽৩

"The whole story is ridiculous, and I don't believe a word of it," Blanche said in a low voice as she leaned across the table. "But I'm guessing you knew that. What I'm wondering is why you're sharing it with me."

I came clean. I had invited Blanche to dinner and told her everything from start to finish about Destiny, Will, Jonathan, Victoria and Zachary Taylor. I hadn't thought she would believe such an outlandish tale. Certainly not. Blanche needed sound, concrete proof of everything—even her own existence. I told her for the exact opposite reason as a matter of fact.

"I told you because I was sure you could come up with a reasonable explanation for everything," I said. I took a small scoop of mac and cheese and pushed the plate to the side. My stomach was in knots.

Blanche furrowed her brow. "Did I hear correctly?"

"Yes," I said, nodding emphatically. "I'm sure you can convince me there's a reasonable explanation for everything that's happened over these past few months. I know I'm not going crazy, and physically, I feel fine."

My sister smiled and shook her head.

"I don't know what to say…"

"What do you mean? You always have a strong opinion about everything!"

Blanche speared a tomato wedge with her fork and twirled it a few inches above her salad as if conjuring up an answer. She carefully chewed and swallowed every last bit of pulp and seed, then looked me straight in the eye.

"Kat, I don't believe these kinds of stories… but this time, I can't come up with a logical explanation. All I can ask is this: Are you sure everything happened as you say it did? Could your interpretation or observation of certain things be skewed? Or could you have confused dreams with reality?"

"I'm not crazy!"

"I didn't say that! I'm simply saying that perhaps certain elements are a bit off... That could be a reason."

"No, I'm sure of my story," I said. "So what do you think of me now?"

"I think there are things in life that can't be explained."

"Have you turned over a new leaf?"

Blanche smiled and rolled her eyes.

"Of course not, Kat. Maybe you're simply finding out something about me that you didn't know."

"What should I do now?"

"I think you should finish up your article, return to New York and forget about all that's happened. Let's imagine the whole story is true. You have two choices: accept that it came to be in order to bring you and Will together, or look at it as another experience that helped you overcome the illness that has plagued you for years. In either case, the outcome is pretty good."

My sister had a way of making sense out of even the most bizarre situations, and she had accomplished the feat yet again.

May 29

I might already have been packing my bags for New York if it hadn't been for Charlotte Moss. She called as I was about to ring the airline to book a ticket on the next flight out. So instead of lugging a suitcase across the airport at four o'clock in the afternoon, I was sitting across from Charlotte and nibbling on a scone with raspberry jam.

Charlotte wrapped herself in a voluminous orange poncho and leaned into the couch's sagging cushions with a sigh. She had something she wanted to tell me, she had said on the phone. But in the 15 minutes since my arrival, Charlotte had spent the whole time preparing a tea tray and fretting about the cold air that snapped through the corners of the old windowpanes.

"It's an unusually cold month of May," she exclaimed over and over as she set out a pot of tea, ran back to the kitchen for the scones, returned, ran back for a pot of cream, and refused my proposals to help.

I took a sip of Earl Grey delicately scented with blue flowers and so did she. Now what? We both looked at each other uncomfortably. Did she know or even care about the story of Victoria Moss? I couldn't bring myself to pronounce the name. Victoria—this inner part of my own self that I still hadn't faced with complete honesty. Thoughts of Victoria frightened me. I had enough trouble understanding my conscious self and the present day. Yet Victoria's role—my role—in the Moss family fascinated me.

Charlotte set down her cup and took a deep breath. I pushed thoughts of Victoria Moss out of my mind.

"I don't quite know if I'm doing the right thing, but I felt I didn't have much choice," she began.

"Is everything OK? I mean, I know things aren't all right, but..."

"Katherine," she interrupted. "It's about the hotel. You see, I told you my sister inherited the second-largest share."

"And you inherited that from her, right?"

She nodded.

"Have the Taylors contacted you about buying it?"

"A lawyer has. I don't know which Taylor he was representing, as they're all very secretive. And what does it matter anyway?"

"You're selling it to them?"

"No, I refused any business dealings with those people. And then I received a second phone call. Another member of Destiny's family, but not from the Taylor side. Someone who seems a bit more trustworthy. So I decided to sell. The sooner the better."

"Do you mind if I ask who's buying?"

"Her name is Gwen Garnier, one of Destiny's cousins."

"Gwen Garnier?" I mumbled. "A French woman? Who coordinates art showings?"

"She is French, but I don't know what she does for a living."

"But how could it be? I didn't think she had that kind of money..."

"You know her?"

"Yeah," I murmured. Gwen had apparently been hiding more from me than I realized.

"As for the money, don't be astonished," Charlotte said, leaning closer and lowering her voice. "Everyone on both sides of Destiny's family is loaded. The difference is I've agreed to do business with the side that's always seemed less fraught with scandal. That's why I immediately gave the nod to the deal with Gwen. It works for both of us. What do you know about her?"

"Only the fact that she's pretty good at keeping secrets. Especially when they're her own."

"What do you mean?" Charlotte asked, wrinkling her brow.

"Nothing." I stood up and dusted crumbs off my lap. "Look, I'm sorry, but I have to rush off. I don't want to be rude, but I have to meet someone. And I might already be too late."

"No worries," Charlotte said, her forehead still wrinkled in consternation. "You'll stop by again for tea?"

But I hardly heard her words as I hurried out the door.

৩৯৫

I held my head in my hands and took several deep breaths as the cab bounced forward on the short journey to Kensington. What did all of this mean? Why had Gwen lied to me? The same questions circled through my head over and over, but each time, I wasn't any closer to finding answers. Was Gwen involved in Audrey's death? Feelings of sadness and fear overcame me. No, I was being ridiculous.

I paid the driver and walked tentatively up the steps to Destiny's front door. The house looked still, lifeless, in spite of the well-tended spots of grass on either side of the front stoop. I rang the bell with every ounce of courage I could muster, but deep within, I knew my effort was useless. Of course Gwen wouldn't be here. She had almost told me as much the last time I saw her. She had no intention of staying on for very long.

"Damn it, damn it, damn it," I hissed under my breath as I slid down to the cold stone and sat for a moment to regroup.

"If you're looking for Ms. Garnier, she's left." A child's voice.

I looked up and directly into the round dark eyes of a girl of about six or seven. Her black hair was braided into two waist-length ropes that swung from side to side as she approached.

"I'm Caroline, and I'm the next-door neighbor," she said matter-of-factly. She held out a small hand for me to shake, then smoothed her denim skirt and sat down next to me.

"Nice to meet you," I said, not knowing quite what to say to this girl who was examining me with bright little-adult eyes. "My name is Katherine and I was... friends... with the lady who used to live here."

"Ah, Destiny! I liked her quite well. She used to give me biscuits, but I had to come over here in secret because Mum and Dad didn't like her. They said she was completely mad, but I thought she was nice." Caroline shrugged her small shoulders and rolled her eyes.

"Then she went away, and there was Ms. Garnier," Caroline continued. "Mum and Dad like her because they say she's the only normal member of the family."

"Oh, so Ms. Garnier and Destiny are relatives?" I bit my lip, hoping this little girl would somehow have information that could help me understand the situation.

"Yes, but Ms. Garnier didn't like people to find out."

"Really? How do you know that?"

"Because she told Mum," Caroline said, her eyes widening in excitement over my interest in her conversation. "Ms. Garnier said Destiny was mad too! And she said that if people found out, they would think she was that way as well—because they're related and everything. I would rather be mad like Destiny than be like boring Ms. Garnier. Mum says Destiny moved away, but I don't believe it. I think Ms. Garnier chased her away."

Then she raised an eyebrow and looked at me eagerly.

"Are you the one who's chasing Ms. Garnier away?"

I couldn't help but smile.

"No, I actually came here to see Ms. Garnier... but she's gone?"

"Yes. She told Mum that she was tired of all the... terchery?"

"Treachery?"

"That's it! The treachery in her family and wanted to be far away from them."

Before I had a chance to say another word, a lilting, high-pitched voice made both of us jump with a start.

"Caroline Elizabeth Acres! What on earth are you doing

over there?"

A 40-something woman with a perfect blond bob slammed the door of her BMW and marched across the sidewalk. She turned to me first.

"Please excuse us for this," she said to me with a fake smile. "Caroline can be a real concierge. I hope she hasn't been bothering you. Her sister was supposed to be watching her." Then she turned a highly annoyed gaze on her daughter, who had already skipped away and disappeared into the house next door.

"Not at all," I said. "I was coming over here to see Gwen... But your daughter tells me she's left?"

The woman's expression relaxed. I had a feeling it was because I said I was seeking Gwen rather than Destiny.

"Yes, she's returned to France."

"Hmm, I thought she was buying a hotel here in London."

"Really! Well, it's true she was always interested in a new business venture. Quite a businesswoman!"

I wanted to ask what she meant by that, as I only knew Gwen's artistic side, but a piercing cry interrupted my thoughts.

"Mum!" The voice of a teenager rang out the front door, followed by a tall, thin girl in jeans. "Caroline is being a pest!"

The woman sighed. "I have to be on my way. Never a dull moment with those two..."

May 30, an early morning hour

Back to The Grand East Hotel. I had left a message on Gwen's cell phone, my only point of contact with her. Would she respond? Only if she believed I had a sudden change of heart and was interested in exhibiting in her next show. I wasn't optimistic though: Gwen wasn't that naïve.

Maybe I could contact her through Will or Dr. Bell... No, I was being ridiculous. Even if I was able to reach her, I couldn't force her to explain the hotel's ownership to me. And what difference would it make anyway? I couldn't prove that Gwen or a member of the Taylor family had anything to do with Audrey's death. Charlotte had accepted her sister's fate. I had to do the same. I promised myself I wouldn't give Gwen or any of her secrets one more thought.

My night was a sleepless one. I lay there, immobilized in bed. Waiting. Waiting for Destiny to whisk me off to another party. But she never came. Waiting for Zachary Taylor to slide into my mind and offer me a glass of champagne. But he never showed up either.

It was over. I would never see them again. I convinced myself of this and was half relieved and half distraught. A strange combination, but entirely possible.

My only reminder of Zachary Taylor would be the earrings still planted firmly in my earlobes, and the hat, carefully wrapped in the dusty shopping bag. And my emotional heritage, from a woman named Victoria Moss.

I got up and ran through the 3 a.m. darkness to the bathroom, turned on the lights and looked into my panicked eyes. Who was this Victoria Moss? Why couldn't I feel closer to her if she was a part of me? Everything felt like an illusion, and then all of a sudden, it felt completely real.

The main question was: Why had Zachary Taylor told me Victoria's last name was Moss? What more could I learn about her or Jonathan after all of the information he and Destiny had given me? I stared into my dilated pupils for I don't know how long until I realized I had to call Charlotte Moss as soon as the clock struck a decent hour. That was why Zachary Taylor had given me the clue. Charlotte must have known something about Victoria that only she could reveal.

✑⤬

Charlotte Moss opened the door—physically and figuratively. She invited me to sit on the now-familiar chair facing the half-open window that always let an unpleasant draft into the little sitting room. She handed me the now-familiar cup brimming with familiar tea and curled up in a corner of the couch to listen to what I had convinced her was an urgent matter.

And, with her large, curious eyes studying me, I hesitated. I hadn't thought of how I would explain this convoluted story to someone who obviously wouldn't believe it. Of course, that had been my situation with Blanche, but she was my sister. I knew she wouldn't throw me out the door or have me locked up.

"What's happened, Katherine?" Charlotte asked, as usual knitting her brow. "Is this about my sister again? Or Gwen Garnier and the hotel?"

"Not really," I began, setting down my cup and taking a deep breath. "At least not directly. It's about the Moss family and something Destiny told me."

"This is about Victoria Moss, isn't it?" she said.

I looked at her in surprise, not knowing how to continue.

"I told you I don't believe the rubbish Destiny and Audrey used to throw around, and I meant it, but they would tell me their stories anyway."

"What did they tell you about Victoria?" I asked, my voice nothing more than a whisper. I trembled and Charlotte reached over to shut the window.

"They told me they found her in the form of an American woman named Katherine."

"Why didn't you tell me you knew about me... being involved in this?"

"Because I don't believe it. I let them go on with their silliness, and I certainly don't have anything against you for believing their stories. We each have a right to our thoughts and opinions. I simply never wanted to get involved and wasn't about to start after meeting you."

She shook her head and sighed.

"I'm not like those in our family who thought Destiny and my sister were crazy. They had their reasons for their beliefs, as we all do. But that's that."

I took a small sip of the tea that had turned lukewarm. Charlotte refilled our cups from the steaming pot and studied me as if weighing her options.

"What is it?" I asked. "Tell me."

She hesitated and then stood up.

"Follow me. I have something I think I should give to you."

She led me up a narrow flight of stairs and into a tiny, pale-pink room crowded with a desk and computer, bookshelves, a loveseat, a chest of drawers and a heap of un-ironed laundry.

"Please excuse the mess," she said, "but I rarely invite visitors up here."

She opened the bottom drawer, fished around toward the back and pulled out a tiny leather-bound book.

"Take this," she said, handing it to me. "It's Victoria's diary."

It was as if the blood had drained from my body as I touched the cover, turned a yellowed page and glanced at the narrow, faded script. I felt dizzy, but using all of the mental power I could muster, I fought the physical urge to faint.

"You don't have to..."

"It's best if you keep it," Charlotte said, putting a hand on my arm. "Really. I've never shown it to anyone, although Destiny and my sister knew I had it and didn't want to give it to them. Maybe I was wrong, but I didn't want to encourage this obsession of theirs."

"But why are you giving this to me if you don't believe?"

"Because I know that you do."

PART III

May 30, later

A day in Victoria's shoes

   Last night, Jonathan gave me beautiful amethyst earrings that I shall wear for eternity. Gently, he fastened them, touched his lips to mine and took a step back as if admiring a painting. He raised one of his perfect eyebrows and winked. I laughed, of course. He joined in, and we soon collapsed onto those old seats in the drawing room that Mother insists on keeping even though they are much too soft. We sank into them and laughed even harder. Mother, who said she had heard us from her dressing rooms, rounded the corner and scolded us for such foolishness at our age. I do not know how we managed, but we held in our laughter until she disappeared out the front door on her way to one of her numerous charity events.

   Jonathan carried me up the stairs, and I melted in his arms as I do each night when we are together. The feeling of his hands unwinding my hair from its rigid knot and untying the ribbons of my heavy gown set me free. I told him I will touch these precious earrings every time he leaves for one of the business trips that I so detest, and by this modest gesture, he will remain close to me. He shall leave tomorrow for a fortnight. I refuse to think of it.

   I wept all morning, but only after Jonathan left. I had not wanted to upset him before such a long voyage. Mother said I was being ridiculous, but I did not care. I told her I was feeling quite ill and needed time alone. That is why I was especially angry when she ordered me into the drawing room to visit with Edward. He was the last person I wished to see. I understood the love-hate relationship between Jonathan and him, the competitiveness between these two brothers who were so very different. Do I dare write on these pages the secret I have never told anyone? Oh, how good it would feel to relieve the suffering by at least expressing it somehow. I cannot resist... Edward tried seducing me last summer as I sat drawing under the weeping willow. He pulled me roughly against him, saying it was impossible for a woman to resist his allure. I did not dare to scream for I knew Jonathan would hear, and I did not want to turn him against his brother. So I did the only thing I could. I kicked him. He nearly screamed, and I started crying, having scared myself with my own aggressiveness. Then I ran blindly into the house, and when Jonathan saw me crying, I told him I had narrowly escaped an attack by a swarm of hornets. Now, I almost laugh as I remember my silly excuse, but when I think back to Edward, fear overcomes me. I shall do anything I can to avoid being alone with him.

Several pages savagely ripped from the little book, as if torn out in a fit of rage.

It cannot possibly be true that Jonathan loves another. I refuse to believe it! Not after his joyous return yesterday, not after that passionate night. "You encounter plenty of beautiful women on your voyages," I said after he whispered "you are beautiful" in my ear. "Do not say such things!" he hissed as if I had struck him. "Jealousy does not suit you, Victoria! You know that I love only you." Then I covered him with kisses and tried to forget the words Edward repeated over and over with each visit. How I despise him!

A few pages about an afternoon in the park with one of Victoria's cousins, followed by beautiful drawings of birds, flowers and then a portrait of a couple I instantly recognized: Victoria and Jonathan, obviously drawn by the young woman herself. My breath caught in my throat as the images matched ones I had seen in my dreams. Jonathan's slim face with a high forehead and almond-shaped eyes, and Victoria, with a haughty gaze and a long rope of curls falling over one shoulder. I stared at the image as if I could somehow penetrate their hearts and minds through it. And then, just as I got too close, I shuddered and turned the page.

I went with him. I did not want to, but he pushed me by force. Oh, I do not know how I can even write with the tears streaming down my face, blinding me. My beloved Jonathan slipping out the door of that brothel. How could it be? How could he do such a frightful thing to us? Edward held me in his arms for so long afterward, but finally, I pushed him away. I did not want anyone's pity.

What could have been old tearstains left strange wrinkled marks on the paper. More ripped pages, obviously torn out with one angry swoop.

God forgive me for what I have done and what I am about to do. I have no choice. I thought he betrayed me, and in the end, I was the betrayer. I was the one without faith in our marriage, without faith in him. How I regret my mistakes, but it is too late. My heart is broken because I have broken his! Jonathan, if you ever read this journal, please know that I love you more than life itself. Please forgive me for hurting you. Everything between us will be over in a few moments... It is better this way.

Victoria's words opened the floodgates that had trembled when I had come to the realization that all Destiny had said was true. This story had been my own, and right at that moment, as I held the diary in my hands, years of suffering flowed down my cheeks in the form of tears.

I had to see Will. How foolish I had been to lie to him and to myself! By turning my back on him, I thought I could escape everything I didn't want to accept. But that was impossible. The story of Victoria and Jonathan would haunt me forever unless I made an effort to put it to rest. And I could only do that by loving Will.

It was time for me to leave The Grand East Hotel. I didn't understand everything that had happened there, but suddenly, it didn't matter. What was most important was rushing back to New York, where I would find the reality I had been blindly seeking for so long.

June 1

There was more to Victoria's diary than those few final excerpts I had read in haste, but after the flood of emotion had overwhelmed me, I decided to take a step back. I'd stuffed it into the bottom of my overnight bag and promised myself I would only read more once I had returned home.

For me, home at this point was the apartment in the East Village. I dropped my bags in the hallway and made a beeline for the shower. It was 10:30 a.m. I had enough time to freshen up and still arrive at Will's gallery by noon. In spite of the exhaustion of an overnight flight, I couldn't think of sleep.

For the first time in a long while, I didn't throw on the first piece of clothing I saw. Instead, I dug through Blanche's closet until I found the lavender empire-waist sundress her ex had bought for her, and she had never worn. I wound my damp hair into a bun, stuck a pencil through it, and with my heart pounding, hurried to the door.

Excitement surged through my veins as I took the steps two at a time and joined the crowd on the Union Square platform for an uptown train. Home. It was so good to be home. But even more than that, the desire to see Will bubbled uncontrollably from within.

Faces of all colors and forms, dim stations, outbursts of laughter and arguments, the sugary scent of one of those coffee-caramel concoctions: All of these familiar sights and sounds repeated themselves until I was exiting at Columbus

Circle and walking, or nearly running, farther uptown. With each step, the feel was more residential, calmer. My heart was still racing, and I was trembling in spite of the hot sun baking dangerously into my pale skin.

And then I had arrived. Too soon and not soon enough. I wouldn't wait a second longer or I would fall victim to the cowardice that would push me back downtown to my safe haven.

I took a deep breath, stepped inside and walked to the counter with as much confidence as I could muster.

"Good morning," said the young woman with perfectly painted red lips that matched her flowing cotton blouse. "May I help you?"

"Hi, I'm looking for Will Delaney."

"Sorry, but he's not in."

"Do you know if I could find him at home?"

"You're the friend of his... the one he met in London, right?"

"Yes, you could say that." I felt heat rising into my face.

The woman smiled uncomfortably.

"What is it?" I asked, almost in a panic.

"Well, I'm not sure I can help you, unfortunately. You see, I'm not sure where he is. He left New York a few days ago. He said he needed some time away and then took off."

"That can't be. I mean, I believe what you're saying, but he can't just take off and leave his gallery indefinitely in the hands of... well, of his employees... without telling them what's going on. He *is* the owner."

"Yes, but so am I. We're co-owners, business partners. Of course, this makes things difficult for both of us."

"He will be back, won't he?" I said, almost to myself. "But when?" I was gripping the counter as if it alone was the only thing that could hold me in an upright position.

"I'd like to think so," the woman said, shaking her head. "He didn't say he was leaving forever. Recently, he seemed distracted, and in the past he's talked about wanting to take a sabbatical. It's not completely unexpected."

"You have no idea where he might be?" I pleaded. "Maybe a clue..."

"Will is such a private person... even being his business partner doesn't give me access to much privileged information. The only thing I do know is that one of his closest friends in London passed away not too long ago. He seemed to be in a daze ever since. Maybe he returned there to visit with friends."

"I saw him in London not long ago," I said. "But he left. He sent me a letter from New York. I guess it's possible he returned, but it doesn't seem likely."

"Look," the woman said, smiling kindly, "how about if you leave me your number, and I'll give him a message when he returns."

"But what if he doesn't return?" I asked, unable to hide the anxiety I must have been wearing all over my face.

Neither of us had an answer to that question.

∽⚬∾

After spending a good part of the afternoon crying my eyes out on Jean's bench in Central Park, I made my way slowly back to the apartment as if I were heading to prison. Through eyes still blinded by tears, I sent my article to the magazine, unpacked my suitcases and threw a load of clothes into the washing machine. I moved through the apartment like a robot, accomplishing every necessary task. It was only when I freed the black hat from its bag that I started crying hysterically yet again. For Will, Zachary Taylor, Destiny, myself... for all of us.

June 3

Three days passed. My only activities had been crying, working on last-minute revisions to my magazine piece, and wondering how, despite the turmoil, I wasn't in the same state of mind I had been in all of my life until meeting Destiny. I no longer had the same kind of problems, I told myself. A small voice in my head reminded me I no longer had the tragedy of Victoria and Jonathan tormenting me from the depths of my soul. But did that really make such a difference?

These were the thoughts running through my mind as I walked toward the front door on my way to meet with my editor. And right then and there, I stopped. An envelope had been tossed through the mail slot, and I had nearly stepped on it. What caught my attention was the handwriting. It was a note from Will.

Kat,

So you see? I was right not to believe you. I heard you were looking for me. I could have easily emerged from this sabbatical of sorts and rushed to meet you on your territory. That's what I would have done a month ago. But after thinking over the situation these past few days, I realized that maybe time apart isn't so bad. More time to reflect on the past and the future... And by the way, welcome back to New York.
Will

I could hardly breathe as the excitement bubbled up. Will

was launching some sort of challenge. I read his message over and over. He was turning the tables on me. Now that I was ready to follow my heart, he was going to make it difficult. This new twist to our relationship set off a spark of intrigue deep within.

I turned over the envelope to look for any clue about its origin, but of course, I found nothing. Someone—maybe even Will himself—had delivered it directly to my door.

He was still in New York. I could feel it.

I threw open the front door and stepped outside as if something there would guide me to him. But at this time of day, I was standing on the sidewalk of a rather sleepy little street with only a few teenagers and their basketball heading to the court a block away. I squinted against the early rays of sunlight and looked around. Will could have been a few feet away in any direction and I wouldn't necessarily be able to find him without looking completely foolish.

"OK, fine," I said aloud. "If you want to know what I have to say, stand by…"

Glancing at my watch, I hurried back inside. If I left in 15 minutes, I wouldn't be excessively late for my meeting. That gave me just enough time to show Will that I wouldn't let him win this little game quite so easily.

Will,

I wasn't ready to fall into your arms, in spite of what you might think. Yes, I was hoping to see you at the gallery, but I was paying you a friendly visit—nothing more. Let's say that my reflections at this point are focused on the lives of Jonathan and Victoria. Maybe one day we can share our knowledge of the subject. You might be amazed at how much I've learned…
Kat

I carefully folded the note into an envelope, addressed it to Will's gallery and slipped it into the mailbox at the end of the street.

June 3, night

Victoria speaks:

I met the man I am going to marry. Mother says I am too much of a romantic, but I do not agree. I am simply realistic and know what I want. There certainly should not be anything wrong with that. Jonathan Hook. I cannot hold back a sigh of ecstasy as I close my eyes and imagine the deep blue gaze that captured me with such intensity.

Zachary brought him to our home for tea yesterday, and as soon as he took my hand, I knew. Does he feel the same? I cannot be sure. Oh, I never seem to have the "feeling" like some girls… My best friend Elizabeth says she can sense these kinds of things immediately. She says my problem is my mother does not invite enough young men to tea, so I do not have the experience necessary to cultivate the "feeling."

Zachary and Mother did most of the talking, while Jonathan and I kept catching each other's eye and smiling. Mother shot me a few sharp looks when our gazes lingered upon each other for what she considered too long. I cried myself to sleep last night, thinking we surely would have nothing but Mother's disapproval. This morning, though, a bit of hope. Mother said Zachary and Jonathan would be returning this afternoon for tea, and that she expected me to attend—and to wear one of my best dresses! That could only mean one thing!

What to wear, what to wear… I spent most of this morning thinking of nothing but how to present myself in the most flattering manner. What if this were to be my only chance to win his attention? My heart raced at the very thought!

Victoria Hook. Victoria Hook. Soon, I would be Victoria Hook.

In my mind's eye, I could see her, and in my heart, I could feel the sense of excitement and nervousness that was overtaking Victoria at the thought of this budding romance. As I read, it was like she was coming back to life.

"My dear Victoria," Zachary told me, taking me by the arm as we walked through the rose garden. "I see you're disappointed that Jonathan didn't accompany me today, but please accept his apologies. He had every intention of coming and every intention of capturing your heart."

"Is that really so?" I exclaimed, turning to him with widened eyes. Then, in a second of panic, I glanced around quickly. To my great relief, Mother was nowhere to be seen. She would have been furious if she heard me engaging in such frank conversation with Zachary—especially about such a subject.

Zachary smiled and patted my hand.

"Don't worry," he said. "Your mother knows and approves. I wouldn't have brought Jonathan here without discussing the situation with her, of course. She finds Jonathan quite acceptable, so if you agree, it is only a matter of time before…"

"When will I see him again?" I asked, my heart now pounding double time.

"Does tomorrow evening suit you?"

I must have fallen asleep at some point during my late-night reading session because the next thing I remember is a dreamlike scene that unfolded in my own mind:

"My dear Victoria, I'm sure you remember my friend, Jonathan Hook," Zachary said as he and Jonathan approached me in the salon where Mother always held her most elegant parties. They both appeared suddenly, almost to my surprise, as they emerged through the mass of familiar characters exchanging greetings and shallow words. The three of us formed a triangle as if in a world of our own, ignorant of the high-pitched voices and a wailing waltz.

"Yes, of course I remember Mr. Hook," I said, trembling as he kissed my hand.

"May I ask you for this dance, Miss Moss?"

"I would be delighted, Mr. Hook," I replied, smiling broadly in a way that Mother frowned upon.

Out of the corner of my eye, I could see Zachary stifling a laugh. He found my rebellious nature quite amusing, which had always encouraged me to take my words or actions one step further just to show him that I truly was capable of shocking Mother. She certainly would find it inappropriate for me to be dancing with Jonathan without even having engaged in a full conversation. But at that point, I was beyond rational thinking. I laced my arm through Jonathan's and walked proudly toward the dance floor.

"I hope I haven't been too presumptuous, Miss Moss," he said as we swirled around as if being carried by a cloud. "I wouldn't want to upset your mother."

"No, Mr. Hook," I said, smiling daintily now, just for him. "Zachary surely is speaking with Mother right at this moment, and maybe we will see them on the dance floor… He gives her dance lessons, as I am sure you know."

"I'm sorry I wasn't able to come to tea the other day."

Our eyes met, locked and would not part.

"A very bothersome business transaction," he said. "But that's taken care of. So tell me, lovely Victoria Moss, would you do me the honor of dancing only with me this evening?"

Heat rose into my face, but I refused to look down in embarrassment. Secretly, I rejoiced at those words I had dreamed of hearing, but I knew I had to keep my composure.

"If that pleases you, Mr. Hook."

June 5

So what have you learned about Jonathan and Victoria? Something that's made you change your mind about us?

I read those lines over and over, my eyes devouring each word. A second note from Will. I had discovered it early in the morning nearly glowing in the sunbeam that crossed the bumpy old hardwoods in the front hall. I studied those lines all morning as a million thoughts ran through my mind: Victoria's diary, my dreams, the reappearance of Zachary Taylor. I couldn't possibly pour out this entire story in a note to Will. Where to begin, and where to end? And it wasn't necessary. After all, Will believed. He believed when I had thought this was a bunch of nonsense.

So rather than answer him in a mundane manner, I decided to try something a bit different...

Dear Will,

You don't really expect me to answer your questions directly, now do you? That would be out of character. Instead, I thought I would tell you a bit of a story. I think you'll find it much more interesting.

Let's say that the following is in Victoria's own words...

The rose bushes were in full bloom, but under the night sky, only the rich scent hinted at their presence.

"These are white," I whispered, afraid of raising my voice and being

caught in this highly dangerous escapade.

*"You must know them by heart to recognize them even in the dark,"
Jonathan replied. I could hear the smile in his voice.*

*"Yes, I spend many afternoons tending to them. Mother prefers the
gardener to take care of the flowers, but I love them so..."*

"Tell me, Victoria, what colors are the next ones?"

*We took a few steps forward, and I shivered slightly in the humid
chill that had blanketed the garden. Jonathan gently squeezed my arm,
but that only made me shiver all the more. After several dances, he had
led me out to the terrace, and then we slipped away from the drunken
couples laughing heartily when hidden by darkness.*

*Alone, in the rose garden. My heart pounded as I turned to face
Jonathan.*

*"These right here are red... the traditional ones," I whispered, my
eyes unable to part from his.*

*"That is my favorite variety," he said, his mouth now brushing
against my cheek. And then he kissed me. Gently, his lips touched mine.
Maybe I should have pushed him away and ran back to the house. An
honorable, decent girl would have done that. But I could not. I did not
want to let him go. Ever. Right then and there, I decided that no matter
what, I would become Mrs. Jonathan Hook.*

*So that's the story, Will. Is this new to you, or have you heard this
one before?*
Kat

June 15

I threw the glossy magazine onto the couch with disgust and tried to wipe away the tears that constantly renewed themselves in my eyes. What did it matter that my article finally made it into print? It was a shell of what it should have been if I had truly wanted to tell the story of The Grand East Hotel. That wasn't the reason for my sadness, however.

Ten days had passed and no word from Will. It was over. After six months of turmoil, of daring to believe in an extraordinary romance, all had vanished as swiftly as it had appeared. In a burst of anger, I grabbed Will's notes off the desk, scrunched them up into one big ball of wrinkled paper and threw them into the trash basket. I could no longer fight the tears. I let them fall freely as I huddled against a cushion and dreamed of days when my biggest problem was not knowing or understanding the reason for my sadness. Ignorance is sometimes bliss.

A tentative jingle at the front door startled me. I jumped up and looked at the clock. It was close to four o'clock. I must have cried myself to sleep. I wiped my bleary eyes and wandered toward the ringing, which now continued more insistently. A package, probably. Blanche was always receiving them, and those delivery guys never liked to leave anything without a signature.

"Just a minute!" I called out impatiently.

With anxious hands, I jiggled the lock and opened the door.

"Sam." The name escaped my throat in barely a whisper.

I stepped back and looked at him through widened eyes.

"I know this is a surprise," he said. "I'm sorry I didn't call first, especially after all this time."

"No... no problem at all," I said, taking him by the hands and leading him inside. I nervously wiped at my eyes and tucked my hair behind my ears. "Excuse me for being such a mess today..."

"It hasn't been easy for you," Sam said. "I understand. That's why I decided to come over and have a chat."

"Sit down," I said, leading him to the couch. "Can I get you anything to drink?"

"No, I'm fine."

We sat facing one another across the coffee table. I bit my lip and studied his calm, kind eyes. He was here to finish the story. The story I thought would never make it to my ears.

"Why did you change your mind... about telling me?" I asked.

"So you know that's why I'm here," he said with a wry smile. "I read your article. I could sense the pain and curiosity you were feeling. Maybe I'm being ridiculous, but that's what I picked up when I read it."

"You were right."

"I guess I should first ask what you know and what you would like to learn..."

"I know what happened to Gabriel and that you resented Destiny for not predicting it. But Sam, I don't understand the parties! We were both there and so was Gabriel! How could he be... gone? And yet we can speak with him. It's like a communal dream!"

Sam hesitated and then leaned closer across the table.

"This is going to be hard for you to believe, but there's no way around it so I might as well say it flat out: They weren't dreams. You know Destiny was a medium. Well, so was Audrey and many of the others who attend those parties. They escort people like you and me, and then they channel the energy. That allows us to experience things we normally wouldn't have the ability to experience. I'm sure you've had a look around the old ballroom before. You've gone up there in the middle of the afternoon, and it's empty. We've all done it. And at first, I have to admit, it would freak anyone out."

"That's how it happened? It was real, after all?" I was shaking so much that Sam grabbed the blanket folded at the edge of the couch and threw it around my shoulders. "For everyone—not me alone. It wasn't only me hallucinating or mixing up fiction and reality! You remember being at the parties, seeing me there, talking with Destiny? Everything?"

"Are you all right? I had hesitated for so long because this is difficult to accept. It seems outrageous, ridiculous."

"I'm fine," I said, touching his arm. "I wanted to hear the details. Of course, it seems impossible! Like the Jonathan and Victoria story. For so long, I didn't know what to believe. Normal people don't accept this kind of thing."

Was I normal? And who defined "normal" anyway? I held my head in my hands and took a few deep breaths.

We were silent for a moment and images of Gabriel's parties raced through my mind one after another. So that's why Zachary Taylor had easily popped up there. Parties that defied time.

As difficult as Sam's story was to swallow, it actually clarified all that had unfolded over the past few months. What other explanation could there be? I had been to those parties and had seen everything with my own eyes. I was perfectly coherent. The same went for Will and Sam. The dream theory didn't hold water, as much as I had wanted to believe it as the one sane explanation. The earrings I still wore and the strange black hat were material proof of my encounters with Zachary Taylor. A feeling of relief overcame me with this piece of the puzzle. My emotional roller-coaster ride was nearing an end.

I looked up at Sam.

"That's how you see Gabriel."

"Yes, it was my deal with Destiny."

"And now that she's gone?"

"There are others who can help me, but the problem is Gabriel is pushing me away."

"I don't understand."

"He doesn't want me to live in the past." Sam stopped and bit his lip. "He wants me to move forward... without him."

"Are you ready for that?"

"No... but I have to force myself to be ready. I'm trying. For the first time, I'm really trying."

I reached across the table and took his hands.

"I'm sorry," I said.

"It's no one's fault... Not even Destiny's. As much as I've blamed her. Just because someone is a medium doesn't mean they don't have limitations. It took me a long while to accept that."

"Are they going to continue?" I asked. "I mean, the parties... without you there. You were the reason Gabriel threw the parties... so that the two of you could be together."

A sad smile lit Sam's eyes and a glossy tear lingered, trapped.

"Gabriel never was very far from a great get-together, and I'm sure there are other people out there who need a late-night spot with a lot of smoke and mirrors as a meeting point."

And then a thought came to my mind.

"Sam, you must have known Destiny's friend Audrey, the girl who died at the hotel not too long ago. She wanted to continue what many people called a lot of commotion at the hotel, and the Taylors were against it. You must know about the Taylors, how they own the place. Then it was for sale, taken off the market..."

"You want to know if Audrey was murdered, don't you?"

"What makes you say that?"

"Because that's what everyone's been asking."

"Well is it true?"

"As if I knew," Sam said, shaking his head. "The story is too complicated. There are too many people with too many individual interests."

"What do you know, Sam?" I pressed on, unable to rein in

the questions I had kept at bay for the past several days. "Did the Taylors kill her?"

"The Taylors haven't had a majority stake in the hotel for years, my dear. They had no reason to kill Audrey."

"What? But that's the complete opposite of what I've heard. Even Charlotte Moss said the Taylors called her to make an offer for the stake she inherited from her sister!"

"Oh, they probably did. Maybe they want to dabble in the business again."

"I don't understand any of this…"

"The Taylors had some financial troubles a few years back so were forced to sell some assets. They did the easiest thing: They sold certain items, including their shares in the hotel, to the other side of the family. A young cousin named Gwen Garnier actually bought up most of the hotel stake. And Destiny of course had a share. Other members of the family purchased paintings and other properties."

"Gwen was a principal owner all along?" I whispered half to myself. "But then why would she put it up for sale and take it off the market? Nothing makes sense!"

"That, I'm afraid, is a question for Gwen Garnier."

"She wanted the parties to stop, and Audrey wanted them to continue," I said, again my voice a shadow of its normal self. "But I can't believe it… She couldn't have…"

I squeezed my knees against my chest and closed my eyes. I didn't want to accept the possibility that Gwen was involved in Audrey's death.

"I've only met Gwen Garnier a couple of times at family parties," Sam said, as if reading my mind. "I don't know her well enough to say whether or not she would do such a thing to clean up the hotel's image and get back to business. It's all circumstantial evidence, in any case."

No proof. One way or the other. I wanted to believe in her innocence. But I wasn't sure I would be able to accept that everything had been simply accidental.

June 15, night

"It's time," the familiar, lilting voice whispered in my ear.

Everything was blurry and spinning, and then suddenly, all was clear. Destiny and I sat across from each other at the table I had occupied with Zachary Taylor as dancers swirled by in colorful costumes. She seemed to glow as her warm hand touched mine and her golden dress reflected the hazel tones in her eyes.

"Time for what?" I felt as if my voice was far, far away, emerging from an unknown part of myself.

"Time to repair the errors of a century ago, of course! That's what this whole story is about, after all. You've already realized that your anxiety and sadness stemmed from a tragic past. Why do you think the depression that drove you to anorexia and suicide attempts disappeared so quickly this time after years of unsuccessfully fighting it? Because you know the truth now! Finally, you know the truth."

"So that's what this was really about…"

"Righting the wrong," Destiny said.

I glanced around quickly, but didn't see any of the usual characters.

"Where are they?" I asked.

"You no longer need them."

❦

I woke up trembling in damp sheets and noted every word, as I knew that I would no longer be meeting with Destiny.

June 16

Dr. Bell's office. He raised a furrowed, gray brow when he saw me enter.

"You look surprised to see me," I said.

"You cancelled our other appointments over the past few months."

"I'm sorry... I was out of town."

"The project with Ms. Garnier? How did that go?"

"Very well. Oh, I can't say that it's a sure cure for someone in my situation, but I think it's helpful. I called her before leaving London saying I would be willing to participate in another project, but I never heard back from her."

Dr. Bell shook his head and scribbled a few words in my file. "That's not surprising," he said. "She's ceased operations."

"Well, that's not surprising, either," I said, "considering she just bought a hotel."

"Yes, she told me. A lifelong dream of hers, apparently."

"You spoke with her?"

He nodded solemnly, set his pen on the desk and sighed.

"She wanted me to relay a message to you."

"Why couldn't she pick up the phone and call me herself? Too ashamed of the lies?"

"You seem upset by the situation with Ms. Garnier."

"I don't want to get into it," I said. "It's a long story, much too long."

"Maybe you'll feel ready to share it another time."

"What did she want to tell me?"

"She sent this note for you," he said, handing me an envelope. "She didn't have your new address. I know you're eager to have a look at it, so if you would like to schedule another appointment with me rather than continue…"

"Yes, thank you," I said, rising hastily. "I'll call you."

But we both knew my time as a patient had reached an end.

Dear Kat,

I know your interest of the past few months has been The Grand East Hotel and all of the stories that have unfolded there. I'm sorry I wasn't able to share the entire truth with you from the start, but as you now know, it's a very messy and complicated situation. And as a result, friends and relatives have transformed themselves into enemies.

A few months ago, I gave up on my dream of bringing this old place back to glory. The parties were too harmful for the hotel's reputation. Then I saw the light at the end of the tunnel, so I jumped on the occasion.

I think almost everyone is satisfied with the outcome. In about six months, the disagreeable and unfortunate events will be forgotten, and visitors will flock to my hotel seeking tranquility—not turmoil in the ballroom. You and Will are welcome as my special guests at any time, and you can be sure there won't be any strange visitors during the night.
All of my best,
Gwen

With shaking hands, I stuffed Gwen's note back into the envelope. She had told me everything and nothing.

June 16, afternoon

"Who was she, anyway?" I asked.

I gently brushed away the dust that once again had been masking her name. There, it shined as brightly as ever on the little bench in Central Park. The lovely Jean.

The man who diligently cared for the plaque with Jean's name sighed, sat down beside me and set his leather bag on the clumps of tattered grass at our feet.

"She fascinates even those who never knew her," he said, half to himself.

"I'm sorry... I don't know why," I said, stumbling over my own words. "It's just that over the past several weeks... things have been difficult. But coming here makes me feel better."

My face was reddening.

"I'm being kind of silly actually," I mumbled. "The idea of imagining this beautiful woman with a zest for life, using her as a point of reference. I know—it's ridiculous. Let's forget about it. I had better be on my way."

I started to get up, but the man put a hand on my arm.

"No, please don't leave. I haven't answered your question."

"You don't have to. I was being nosy."

"Not at all."

I sat down tentatively at the edge of the bench.

"She was one of my patients... but she was more than

that too. She left us a few years ago—much too early. But I don't want to focus on that. It's best to focus on her life. An extraordinary young woman. She was a photographer and traveled the world snapping shots of wildlife. She had set up a gallery with her dear friend Will, and they displayed their work."

"Did you say 'Will'?" My voice caught in my throat. I knew. Now I knew why I kept coming back to this bench.

"Yes, his gallery is right here in the neighborhood. He kept it going, but took on another business partner."

"I think I know him," I said. "Will Delaney."

"Yes, that's it. And you happened upon this bench one day? By accident?"

I nodded.

The doctor grinned.

"She still never ceases to amaze me," he said, again almost to himself.

My mind was racing. Who had led me to this bench anyway? Was it Jean herself? Could it have been Destiny? She must have known Jean. All of these forces from beyond kept pushing me in the same direction. And finally, I was ready to listen.

One more chance. That's what we have. If you want to take me up on it, I'll be waiting on Jean's bench in Central Park. Don't ask me how I know. I just do. I'll be there at 5 p.m. tomorrow.

That was the note I slipped into Will's mailbox. He was home. I was sure he hadn't left the city for a minute.

June 17

I wandered around Central Park for an hour to kill time. In a daze, I walked around the back of the Met, down the sloping valleys, past the sunbathers spread across the grass, around my favorite pond and then slowly made my way to Jean's bench. My heart should have been pounding a mile a minute, but it wasn't. Strangely enough, a sense of calm had overcome me.

I glanced at my watch. 4:55 p.m. The designated meeting spot was empty. I walked steadily toward this now-familiar bench, whose only occupants were a few leaves brought there by a gust of wind. A thin film of dust covered the name plate yet again. I kneeled on the seat, and with the edge of my skirt, polished Jean's name until it shined.

"Housekeeping, are we?"

Will. My heart skipped a beat. I took a deep breath and turned around.

He was smiling and took me by the hands. In a second, I collapsed into his arms, and both of us sank onto the bench that cradled us in the late-afternoon sun. His lips on mine were vaguely familiar, but to my surprise, all thoughts and images of Jonathan and Victoria had drifted away. Will was like a new discovery.

Jonathan and Victoria had served their purpose as the vehicle necessary to bring the two of us together. The idea that this old, tragic story was beginning to detach itself from us filled me with a sense of relief.

"They're gone," I whispered into Will's ear.

"What do you mean?" he asked, smiling coyly.

"You know... Jonathan and Victoria. The whole story. I can't feel it any more! Those images that haunted me. Is it the same for you?"

Will nodded. "Ever since I started looking toward the future rather than the past."

୨•୧

So that's my story, *our story*. I would probably never understand everything that had happened over these past six months or be able to explain to anyone how my years of suffering had disappeared almost effortlessly. It was much too vague and illogical. The cast of characters was all too incredible.

But as long as Will and I believed in destiny, what else mattered?

Acknowledgements

I would like to thank my husband Didier for his encouragement and support, and his faith in me and my writing career: You have kept me going even during the toughest times. And a special hug for my daughter Phèdre—your patience surpasses my expectations.

A thank you to T. and N., who brought Gabriel and Sam to life for me. That sort of inspiration is one of the best gifts you can offer a writer.

Merci to Valérie Ferrière of the U.S. Embassy in Paris for giving me a chance and helping me to reach out to new audiences.

Thank you to my friend, fellow author and business partner Vicki Lesage for jumping into the adventure of Velvet Morning Press with me. You are a dream to work with!

And thanks to formatting expert Ellen Meyer who made *Close to Destiny* look so lovely.

Finally, as I see *Close to Destiny* on the bookshelf, I thank my dear Auntie Jean for adding magic to my life.

About the Author

Adria J. Cimino is an author of contemporary literary fiction and a partner in the boutique publishing house Velvet Morning Press. She lives in Paris with her husband and daughter..

Adria hopes you enjoyed *Close to Destiny*! If you did, please consider leaving a review on Amazon. Even a few sentences can help future readers decide to pick up the novel.

Want more? Get Adria's short story *Flore* for free! Simply join her new release mailing list: http://bit.ly/cimino-news.

To follow Adria's latest adventures in Paris or learn about her upcoming books and writing projects, visit AdriaJCimino.com.

Adria's other books include:

Paris, Rue des Martyrs, a novel that paints an intriguing picture of the intertwining relationships of four strangers in Paris.

Before Paris, a short prequel to *Paris, Rue des Martyrs*.

That's Paris, an anthology of fiction and nonfiction stories about living, loving and surviving in the City of Light.

Legacy, an anthology that asks the question: What will you leave behind?

Read on for a sneak peek of *Paris, Rue des Martyrs*...

An intriguing encounter at…

Flore

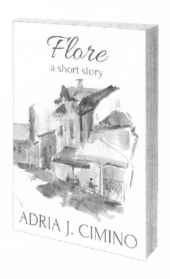

Apolline has tea at Café de Flore in her chic Parisian neighborhood every week with her mother and grandmother. But today, after the teatime routine, she dares to return alone… for an intriguing encounter.

"Flore" is the first in a series of Café Life stories by Adria J. Cimino. In this volume, it is accompanied by "Love Unlocked," one of the author's stories from the anthology *That's Paris*.

Get it for free! Join Adria's new release mailing list and she'll send you a free ecopy of *Flore*: http://bit.ly/cimino-news.

Paris,
RUE DES MARTYRS

A Novel

Chapter 1

Rafael

Rafael Mendez arrived like a thief in the night at 120 Rue des Martyrs. He ran all the way from the train station, where he had left one small, ragtag suitcase in a rented locker. His sneakers slapped noisily along the cobblestones, then pavement, in time with his own tears and the rain falling from a grim Parisian sky.

It was as if each minute lost counted for everything in his 23-year-old life. He pushed past umbrellas that seemed to tango as they bobbed against one another, old men who chatted with no one in particular, couples laughing, and a few sidewalk café tables left behind to weather the storm.

He was nearly blind to this first vision of the city, and only looked up now and again at the street signs to reassure himself that—yes—he hadn't lost the Rue des Martyrs. And then he stopped. He pushed wet strands of long, black hair back from his face, wiped away the silly tears of that odd combination of desperation and excitement, and sank down onto a bench facing the address he had imagined all of his life in Colombia.

Now, as the rain soaked through his jeans and his gaze traveled across the street to the only lighted apartment in building 120, his mind returned home. That's where his quest began, after all. In Bogotá.

৩৯৫

As a child, he would play with the emeralds. That was his first memory. Not mother. Not father. Emeralds. Because that was how his life began. His father never wanted to tell Rafael that the French jewelry designer gave birth to him on a trip for those precious stones. He only said it once—grimly—shaking his head and staring at the dark sand under their feet. Rafael remembered looking up at him with widened 10-year-old eyes as they plodded along the dusty trail to where his father would buy the stones. It was Rafael's first trip there with his father, and in the young boy's mind, it became a sacred place.

But he couldn't think of that story right now or those fucking emeralds. It was over. He had to erase every memory from his mind, the images that haunted him at night.

The one remaining light in 120 snapped off, leaving the building in darkness. It would be too late. He was wasting time. His heart raced as he crossed the street between the cars that kicked up muddy water onto his jeans. He ignored the honking horns. He wanted to move forward, and all at once he wanted to travel back. Rafael was frightened. Afraid of what he might learn or might not learn. Never be afraid, his father had hissed into his ear on that first trip for emeralds.

Before he could let his worries swallow him up with one great gulp, he pounded his fist on the heavy, brown-lacquered door that like a clamshell closed the apartments to the world. Nothing. The sound of his fist against the wood reverberated through his entire body, but no one responded. He scolded himself for his own impatience. How could he possibly have expected someone to answer that door at 11 o'clock on a Thursday night? He placed his hand softly against the handle and sighed, knowing he should leave, yet not able to abandon the glimmer of hope that his problems would be resolved in a matter of hours.

The door creaked open suddenly, and he jumped back.

"There's no need to be startled, you know. When you knock on a door like a maniac, you should expect it to open."

A wispy redhead slipped through the doorway and onto the sidewalk. She gave him a crooked grin, lit a cigarette and leaned against the cool brick.

"So," she said, blowing smoke to the sky, "who do you

want to see that badly?"

Something about the young woman struck him. She wasn't beautiful, with her almost pasty complexion and skinny figure in oversized jeans, but she had an assertive air about her that was much more impressive.

"It must be pretty serious," she continued, taking a drag. "Why don't we talk about it?"

"Do you know a woman named Carmen?" Rafael asked, his voice shaking.

"No."

"Someone named Carmen lives or lived here..." he said, his words trailing off. He felt ridiculous and unprepared as he faced such inquisitive eyes.

"A lot of people have been around here," she said. "I need specifics."

"That's the problem. I don't have any."

"What have you come here for anyway?"

"Answers."

She flicked her half-smoked cigarette into the gutter and with green eyes paler than any emerald gazed up to the sky.

"What are your questions?"

A window flew open from above and a woman's voice called out: "Laurel? Laurel..."

The person who had to be Laurel pulled Rafael against her and ducked into the shadows. She grinned mischievously.

"I've got to run."

His heart skipped a beat as her hair brushed against his cheek. But he kept any flicker of sentiment in check. He didn't have time for distractions.

"Meet me back here tomorrow—same hour," Laurel whispered. "I'll see what I can find out. I have some connections..." And then she slipped away from him and into the night.

Find out what happens next... buy *Paris, Rue des Martyrs* today!

CPSIA information can be obtained at www.ICGtesting.com
Printed in the USA
LVOW11s0900151115

462644LV00001B/82/P

9 780692 346945